Praise for Jeremy Jordan King

Night Creatures

"*Night Creatures* is quite simply, a brilliant and moving read. *Night Creatures* again establishes Jeremy Jordan King as a strong voice in LGBT fiction and one worth watching out for."—*SoSoGay*

"[A] unique contribution to the growing corpus of YA-LGBT titles."—*Foreword Reviews*

In Stone

"If King keeps coming up with such intriguing premises, I'll keep buying his next books."—*Lambda Literary*

D1713978

By the Author

In Stone

Night Creatures

Dark Rites

DARK RITES

by

Jeremy Jordan King

A Division of Bold Strokes Books

2015

DARK RITES

ISBN 13: 978-1-62639-245-8

This Trade Paperback Original Is Published By
Bold Strokes Books, Inc.
P.O. Box 249
Valley Falls, NY 12185

First Edition: February 2015

Credits
Editor: Jerry Wheeler
Production Design: Stacia Seaman
Front Cover Illustration by Jeremy Jordan King
Cover Design by Sheri (graphicartist2020@hotmail.com)

Acknowledgments

First, I must thank my family for encouraging a love of the arts, both fine and magic. My father's library of strange and wonderful books has always been a source of inspiration, but it was especially helpful in the creation of this book. My mother's dedication to exposing her children to theater gave these characters a world to live in.

Thanks to my editor, Jerry Wheeler, for quickly diving into this series and for making the process of refining this story shockingly smooth. To the Bold Strokes team, you're all great and just like…really, really cool people. Thanks for existing.

And thanks to everyone who read snippets of this story and the ones that came before it. I'm glad you liked Rita enough in the first two novels to give me a reason to write a third one all about her.

To my sister, Kelley.
Besides Rita, you're the most magical woman I know.

These metaphysics of Magicians
And necromantic books are heavenly:
Lines, circles, scenes, letters, and characters:
Ay, these are those that Faustus most desires.
O what a world of profit and delight,
Of power, of honour, and omnipotence
Is promised to the studious artisan!
All things that move between the quiet poles
Shall be at my command: Emperors and Kings
Are but obeyed in their several provinces,
Nor can they raise the wind or rend the clouds;
But his dominion that exceeds in this
Stretcheth as far as doth the mind of man.
A sound Magician is a mighty god.
Here, Faustus, tire thy brains to gain a Deity.

—Marlowe's *The Tragical History of Doctor Faustus*

Spring 1923

His metronome legs swung in a 4/4 time signature, the same as the music he'd rehearsed that morning. As he walked through Midtown and listened to his footsteps, he couldn't help relive the experience. Step, step, step, step translated to "Once I loved you..." The next four beats of his feet meeting slick pavement matched the next line, "Oh, how that's changed..."

How common.

Common lyrics, common themes, common melody, common tempo. He recalled a moment while practicing when it all clicked, when he decided he could do it. *I hate this music. I hate these people.* Then he continued plunking out notes, but with more vigor. More violence.

He stalked across Sixth Avenue with equal strength. The heels of his shoes clicked the ground with such force, he thought he might leave a wake of potholes for unsuspecting chorus girls to fall into on the way to their calls. If they stumbled and broke their necks, they'd be spared the inferno waiting for them at curtain. He felt some relief in that.

Then he adjusted the parcel under his coat. Didn't want gunpowder on his new vest.

If he was going to blow up the theater, why did he even bother spending the first several hours of his day going over music with sixteen screeching beauty queens? Because, even though his mental state had withered, Salvatore was trying to get back into a routine—appear more healthy—and playing piano for those hungover canaries every morning at ten o'clock was part of it. After that, he took lunch at noon, read between two and three, napped until five, ate at five thirty, then exercised at six before he had to be back at the theater for a performance.

This long stroll down Forty-Third Street would have to count as the latter, even though he didn't consider walking proper exercise. He'd always been too thin, so he was more interested in weight training. A strict set of push-ups and squats was necessary to acquire the physique he desired—the one seen in photographs on the walls of that speakeasy on Thirty-Seventh and Seventh. *That* body was the opposite of the lithe one he possessed, the one he wanted to get in top shape for Vincent. Trekking clear across town wouldn't do much for bulking up, but it would relieve his fears of developing a stomach like all the men on his father's side. And the cool air would clear his head.

You don't need to do this, Sal, said a voice inside his mind.

He shook it away, stepped into a doorway, and lit the last of his cigarettes. He was careful not to bring the lighter too close to the explosives hidden under his coat. After all, this wasn't a suicide mission. He was doing this to teach them a lesson.

CARRIE

Spring 1910

Carrie tried not to let horror show on her face. She felt fear in the back of her ribs, like a hand had grown from the chair, clawed through her skin, and gripped bone. Her breathing became faint and her head light. She attempted to swallow the sensations, to suppress the urge to scream or weep, but her throat had become parched. Her hand shook as she brought a teacup to her lips. The sip did nothing for her nerves. "It seems like you had a rough one, my dear," she said to the little girl sitting across the table. The transatlantic voyage had left the child a fright, almost feral looking.

"Yes, ma'am," the girl replied. Her fingernails crusted with dirt, she reached for the cake her aunt had made especially for her.

"Here. Let me help you with that." Carrie slid the plate in her direction and stood to serve a square. The girl smiled gratefully. That gesture momentarily made Carrie forget the troubles surrounding her niece. She became just a tiny thing again, a six-year-old that had been an American for mere hours. "Is it tasty, Margarite?"

Her mouth was full. "Yes, ma'am." Clumps of powdery sugar clung to her lips. She popped her pointed tongue between them to catch the sweet bits. Again, she smiled.

Carrie blushed. "You don't have to call me that. I'm no stranger. I'm your *auntie*."

Another grin, this time showing her teeth. Several of them were missing. She was at the age where all children look like jack-o'-lanterns. The girl glanced to her right to get permission from her mother. "All right, *auntie*. Mum's said so."

Carrie clenched her jaw. She looked wearily at the filthy girl in front of her. She was an absolute shell of the happy child she'd imagined. Those ships weren't the cleanest, especially for a widowed mother and daughter traveling in third class, and somehow the poor thing had caught bugs. Her shiny raven hair had been sheared off to prevent the spread. "Positively medieval," she whispered to herself. Margarite glanced up, as if she were being addressed. Carrie smoothed her smock. "We should get you washed up, child. I have to be at work in a bit. Miss Mabel is going to look after you next door. I'll just be a little while."

"But Mum's here. She can watch me."

Carrie bit her lip, took a breath, and tried to find a delicate way to speak to such a fragile child. "Your mother is tired from the journey." Margarite reached a hand for her mother, but Carrie snatched it. "You'll go to Miss Mabel's."

❖

That evening after Carrie returned from work, she found her niece sleeping at the foot of her neighbor's bed. "How's she been, Mabe?"

Mabel, a red-faced Irish woman with clear blue eyes, was

drying dishes with a ragged cloth draped from her belt. "Oh, she's a sweet girl, she is. Quite an imagination. Busied herself for several hours. Didn't even touch Johnny's old toys."

"That's good. Yes." Carrie watched her sleep. Curled up like that in the dim light, she looked like the angel-child she'd expected to pick up at the dock. "I was firm with her earlier. I feel badly. I hope she doesn't resent it."

Mabel put down the dish and walked to her friend. "Oh, Car. Havin' a wee one like that 'round isn't easy. Especially for you, what after bein' alone for so long. You'll get there."

Carrie looked at her crossly.

Mabel swatted her with the rag. "You know what I mean, ol' girl. The only pitter-patter of li'l feet you hear is from down the hall. You wouldn't know what to do with a bird in a cage that came with instructions, let alone a human being after a voyage through Hades. She's a delicate thing."

"I know, I know. It's just that..." Carrie stumbled for words. "Sometimes I'm scared of her." She looked shyly at Mabel, expecting to hear a laugh.

"Of course you are!" She nudged Carrie. "Children can be terrifying things. An' no worry. Her hair will surely grow back." She unsuccessfully muffled a laugh and had to catch it in her shoulder.

Carrie knocked her with her elbow and chuckled along. "Hush! You'll wake her."

Mabel shook her head like it wasn't an issue. "Oh, poor thing'd sleep through a raid. No worry." She shuffled back to the washbasin and picked up a mug. "How was the show tonight, love?"

"The diva didn't pop a stitch, if that's what you're asking. Yeah, it was good."

"Your clothes are very pretty, Car, but I don't understand

why anyone would want to sit and watch some cow sing Italian for four hours. Do those people in the audience even know what she's saying up there?"

"Oh, probably not. But it is pretty. Very beautiful music. I don't quite understand myself, so I just close my eyes and let the sound carry me away."

Mabel rolled her eyes. "I don't think that's how it's supposed to work, but whatever gets you through the day is fine by me. Now why don't you carry off that wee one so I can get some rest? Johnny's bringin' some new girl to lunch tomorrow, so I'll need to clean from here 'til kingdom come. I'm hopin' she'll settle him down right quick."

"He has been running around for years, hasn't he?"

"Yeah, yeah. But he's a good boy." Mabel looked at Margarite. The sight of the girl relaxed her face and allowed her eye to find a twinkle. "And she's a good girl. Goin' to be pretty, I can tell. You'll have your hands full with those looks when the time comes. Good luck to you, love."

From the looks of that child, Carrie couldn't believe she'd grow up to be beautiful. But she couldn't believe a lot about that girl. She hoped she'd understand her soon.

❖

Carrie lay Margarite down in her bed. She had an impulse to smooth her hair—she'd seen mothers do that to children—but something about how it'd been chopped off made her skin crawl. That and she wasn't her mother. Maybe an auntie would simply pat her on the back.

"Have we made it yet?" the girl groggily asked.

Carrie hadn't meant to wake her. She felt a panic. "No, no, child. You're already here. In America."

"In New York?"

"Yes. In New York. With your Auntie Carrie." That tiny smile returned. It made an equally tiny tear come to Carrie's eye. She never thought her name would bring a smile to the face of a child. The idea made her so happy, she did something she wouldn't have dreamed of doing several hours prior. "If you'd like, you can sleep with me tonight, dear."

Margarite's eyes went from crescents to full moons. "I'm going to sleep with Mum."

"Darling, you can't sleep with your—"

Before she'd a chance to tell her to stay, Margarite fled to the other room.

❖

Carrie stared at the ceiling for what felt like hours. The day had been draining, but sleep wouldn't come.

That girl. She's more than she asked for.

That girl. So attached to an absent mother.

That girl. Her tiny accent made her miss the home she fled many years ago.

That girl. Reminded her she wasn't young.

That girl. Like the little one she'd yearned for.

That girl. Had her mother's eyes.

That girl. Had Marcus's face.

That girl. Was everything she ever wanted but could never have.

That girl. A second chance.

The next day, she'd bring that girl to the park and try to fall in love with her.

❖

Carrie heard about a pond in Central Park that was becoming quite famous for model yacht races. She thought it would be the perfect place to take Margarite. After all, what child wouldn't enjoy a park? And a park where even adults play with toys? It was a guaranteed success. The outing unfortunately took longer than anticipated, for all Carrie knew about the pond was it was called the Conservatory Water and it lay off Fifth Avenue. The long walk from the tenement district of Hell's Kitchen to the luxurious neighborhood of palatial town houses near the park was both tiring and emotional for Carrie.

She despised the neighborhood she lived in—a filthy row of streets ridden with sad immigrants and tyrannical gangsters. Having a child in hand made her even more aware of how terrifying it was. Usually she only had herself to fend for. In the ten years she'd lived on that island, she'd mapped the safest routes and mastered the art of deflecting lewd calls and threats. Her pace was typically quick, and her demeanor dark. But Margarite slowed her down and forced her weaknesses to bubble to the surface.

When they finally arrived at the watering hole, Carrie felt frazzled and ugly. The families nearby were well dressed and groomed. Men wore coats and women pastels. Their hair was pinned and perfect, while her red hair stuck out of a depressing brown hat like blazing pieces of straw. Her cheeks and nose had flushed to a matching rouge, and her freckles were made dark from the sun overhead. She hadn't felt that foreign in ages and wished to have access to the same French cosmetics those women wore. She reached into her bag and pulled out a handkerchief, blotted her skin, and tried to ignore their snickers.

Outside she smiled at the pleasant spring day, but inside

she berated herself for even thinking she'd feel comfortable being such a person in such a neighborhood. And with such a child! She nearly forgot about the imp she walked with. Margarite stood at the edge of the pool, staring at the boats zooming by. Carrie's heart raced. She had to get her away before the others believed her to be an escapee from an asylum or religious cult. She reached for Margarite's hand. "Darling, we have to go."

"Do you think my hair will grow back red, like Mum's?"

"I can't say, child. We have to—"

"And like yours."

There it was again. Another moment of budding affection that made Carrie melt. Several times now Margarite had smiled or glanced or moved or spoken a certain way to make her crack. *And like yours.* That sentence and the accompanying expression were a perfect amalgamation of reasons to feel for the child.

She looked just like him.

"Your father's hair was red, too. Very red. Like the top of a match."

"I want to have his hair, then."

Carrie kneeled down and touched her crudely chopped locks. "Your pa's mum had dark hair just like you. You're more like him than you think."

Margarite half-smiled. "But how will I know if I'm like him if I don't even know what he looked like? He's dead, you know." She spoke as if it were a well-known fact written alongside dates of wars in textbooks that Carrie had forgotten to study.

Carrie blanched, her eyes flooded, and her neck became tight with an oncoming sob. "I know, little bird." She touched Margarite's cheeks. "I know." Her head bowed for three seconds as she fought through sadness, then she brought her niece back to the edge of the water. "Look in there. See your reflection?"

The girl nodded.

"Make some silly faces at yourself. With your mouth."

Margarite giggled and then followed the instructions. She scrunched it into a kissy face, bared her teeth, stuck out her tongue, and blew air through her lips.

"Yes." Carrie laughed. "Those are the same silly faces your pa used to make. You have his mouth." She pointed at the reflection. "And here, you have your mum's eyes."

Margarite gasped. "They're your eyes, too. You're her sister!"

"You're a smart one, you are." Carrie grinned larger than she had grinned in some time. She felt her skin crack in places that had so long sat stationary. When she worked through that tightness, she exercised more muscles by smiling even greater.

"When we get home, you, me, and Mum will stand in front of the mirror and point out our likes."

Car's clown smile drooped. "You know we can't do that, dear."

"Why not? I'll just ask her when we get back."

"No. Margarite."

"Or maybe she's near. She followed us part of the way. I saw her. She didn't want me to tell you because you always say—"

"Love, stop." That firmness was back in her voice. She tried to soften her tone. "Let's get a candy from the shop."

"You always say she's tired." Margarite stomped her foot. "You won't let me see her, but she wants to. She wants to see me."

"You can't be with her now. You can't see her."

"You're just saying that because you're jealous."

"Little bird, that's not true. It's time to go."

"It is. It is true. You're jealous and won't let me see Mum because you loved Pa."

Carrie's blood ran cold. Even the sun seemed embarrassed and hid behind a cloud after such an accusation. "Who's told you such things?"

Margarite stood solidly, her face firm as stone.

"Margarite!"

"Mum! Mum told me. She said that's why you left home. You were mad he married her and not you."

"That's not true." Carrie spat through gritted teeth. "That's not true at all."

Margarite erupted. "It is true. Mum told me. She never lies. She told me last night."

Carrie scanned the perimeter of the pool. The fancy ladies and gentlemen were looking at her and the wild child she'd brought in. She gave her a stern look. "You need to calm down, girl. Stop making up stories."

"They're not stories," screamed Margarite. She kneeled down, picked up a handful of murky water and splashed it into her aunt's face. Their audience gasped.

Carrie, too riled for social graces, shrieked as the spray hit her. "Margarite!"

The girl scampered away through the shallows of the pool and ran back toward Fifth Avenue.

Carrie stumbled as she chased after her, but her niece was too fast. She lost her. As she stood dumbfounded at the mouth of the park, she was sure she heard people make rude comments about keeping dogs on leashes. Maybe she should have got one for her little animal.

❖

"Was that your girl I saw strolling by earlier, Car?"

She lifted her head. By that time, her hat had been lost and her hair was an untamable wildfire in wind. Old Delenie Cross was smoking his pipe on the corner, probably been there all day hollering at young ladies as they passed. But he never spoke to Carrie out of turn. She'd been buying fruit from him for years. "You saw her? You saw Margarite?"

"If that's the same little lady I saw you walking with this morning, then yes. I saw her pass about an hour or so. Went into your building."

There wasn't two cents about her to even thank the man; she darted directly for her home. She climbed the five flights to the top floor. The door was open. Just as she was about to start yelling, she heard crying.

"I told you I was. I'm sorry, Mum."

Carrie stepped in the doorway.

"I didn't mean to, Mum."

She peeked her head around the corner. She could see Margarite sitting at the table, looking across at someone.

"She don't like me. I want to go home. I want to see my friends."

Finally, Carrie came into full view and spoke up. "Who you talking to?"

Margarite jumped. "I'm talking to Mum."

Carrie stepped into the room and walked cautiously to the table. She pulled out the chair opposite her niece.

Margarite stood. "What are you doing?"

"I'm sitting with you."

"No!" The girl pushed her chair backward. "Mum's here with me. It time for us. Just us." Margarite's rage cooled, and she leaned over the table. "Don't worry, Mum." Her face changed. "Mum?" She pounded her hand on the table. "Mama, speak. What's wrong?"

Carrie desperately tried to hold back tears, but this display was too intense. She choked once on sorrow, gasped for air, and left the room.

That girl. That poor girl.

❖

"Carrie! Carrie, my dear!" called Lenora as she practically ran down the hall to meet her. "This...this wing *thing* keeps tangling with my dress." She held up her arm, which had a sheer piece of fabric draped from her wrist to her back.

Carrie's face blanked with irritation. "You're playing an air spirit. If you keep your arms up, like Mr. Stern instructed, it won't rub with the gems on your dress. See?" Carrie demonstrated. She held the actress's arms up, displaying the swirls of colors dyed into the cloth.

"Am I expected to keep them elevated all evening? I haven't the strength for that."

A short man wearing pieces of velvet cut to resemble a cluster of leaves marched by. "Oh, Nora," he said. "Stop your pissing and hold your goddamned arms up for the twenty minutes you're onstage. It's just a song-and-dance show." He held up a bunch of knotted white hair. "Do you have the gum for my beard, Car?"

"Of course, Herb," she said. She reached into her multi-pocketed apron. "You have a good show."

He was about to thank her, but Lenora cut in. "It isn't just a *song-and-dance show*, Mr. Witherspoon. It's an opera. And a very important one at that."

He exhaled in Carrie's direction, his way of not so discreetly communicating frustration about his co-star. Carrie turned her head to hide her smile. "Honey, I'm playing a gnome. You're playing a fairy. I wouldn't call this high art."

The two began to bicker, and Carrie excused herself. As she made her way down the hall, she reached her hand into a clothing rack. She pulled out a black belt...and Margarite. "I told you to wait in the room." She hurried the girl back toward the stairwell.

"I wanted to see the ballerinas."

"Last I checked, there weren't any dancers in between kickers and stockings." Margarite appeared sad. Carrie stopped and kneeled. "If you want to see something, just ask. This isn't the place for little girls to be running around. We'll both get in trouble."

Her niece smiled that smile again. She began to wonder if the girl knew it was the perfect way to her heart. Still, she had to get Margarite out of the halls. It wasn't a written rule, but children were discouraged from being backstage at the opera house. But with the evening performances and erratic rehearsals, many employees brought their young ones with them. Management generally turned a blind eye as long as they were kept out of sight. Carrie hated flirting with regulations, but Mabel had an appointment and couldn't watch the girl. It was the only choice.

As they descended the stairs to the costume level, Mr. Stern, the director of that evening's performance, was walking up. Carrie felt a panic rise in her chest. He had a tendency toward grumpiness, and she didn't want him complaining to the higher-ups about a short-haired child wandering around. She gripped Margarite's hand a bit too tightly.

"My girl!" exclaimed Mr. Stern.

Carrie exhaled her fright and let an awkward grin creep across her face. Mr. Stern had never been especially warm to her. Possibly he was in a strangely jolly mood because it was opening night? Or he was drunk. Either way, she had to match his excitement. "Good evening, Mr.—"

Margarite instantly struggled from her grip and jumped down the stairs to meet him. She stopped several steps above him and extended her hand.

Mr. Stern looked queerly at her.

Carrie's head became light. She'd rather faint than face the embarrassment.

Then the director broke out in a huge toothy grin. He laughed three times to himself, and shook Margarite's hand. "Quite the girl you have, Ms. Connor."

Carrie's mouth hung open, unable to find words. Eventually all she could do was walk down and put a firm hand on the girl's shoulder. "Mr. Stern…I'm…I'm…I apologize for Margarite. She's—"

"What for? She's a lovely child." He rubbed her messy hair. "I shouted at the poor thing in the crosswalk earlier. Seems I mistook her for a little boy, what with this haircut you've given her." Carrie blushed. "Well, let me tell you, she's a little spitfire. She let me know right quick that she wasn't a boy. I received quite the scolding."

Carrie turned her niece to face her. "Margarite."

"No worry, Ms. Connor," Mr. Stern said. "There's no offense. It's nice seeing children around who are interested in the theater."

"I met ballerinas," Margarite lisped through missing teeth.

Mr. Stern kneeled down to her level. "Yes, you did!" He rose to meet Carrie. "You should enroll her in the dance course. Mrs. Lane is in charge of the children's chorus. Maybe she can play an angel in *Hansel and Gretel* next season."

"Please! Please, Auntie!" Margarite was jumping up and down, flaunting her strategically adorable face.

Carrie erupted in giggles. "Yes, of course."

"Once her hair grows out, that is." He grinned for a

moment, then leaned in to speak. "The girl also tells me her mother is a seamstress."

Margarite cut in. "She is! She is!"

"Well, if she is in need of employment, Mr. Fellows at the *other company* needs workers."

Carrie's eyes widened.

"Competition aside, James Fellows is a friend, and he asked I keep my ears open for potential costumers." Mr. Stern peered around, lowered his voice. "Besides, it will just be temporary employment. I wager they'll fold within the year. That's classified information, of course."

Carrie awkwardly curtsied. "Yes, Mr. Stern."

While the director said good-bye to Margarite like one would say good-bye to a small fluffy dog, Carrie decided she needed to get help.

❖

Carrie had heard about things like Spiritualism, séances, and other supernatural practices, but she didn't really understand them. She usually allowed her mind to wander away from conversations like that. Even though she didn't consider herself a religious woman, a childhood of regularly attending mass left her superstitious. Now that Margarite was proving so difficult for her, Carrie regretted not learning more about the things that gave her the spooks.

She wished she had the name of a medium or witch doctor or priest of some strange order to educate her. Instead, she'd have to ask around. Luckily this wasn't too difficult a task because the city had recently been through a brief obsession with sensational beliefs. When Carrie came over ten years ago, she had read somewhere that New York City had over one hundred businesses focused on these flights of fancy. Those days were fading away, but more than a handful of ladies with crystal balls were still floating around.

"My stars!" squealed Patricia, a chorus girl being fitted for a new corset. "You *must* go to Elisabeth!"

Carrie's face reddened with her every word. "Keep it down," she whispered. "No need to announce to the whole cast." She pulled the strings a little too tight to make a point. Patricia squeaked.

A man without pants walked in. "Getting your fortune told, Carrie?"

"No, Marlo. I'm not. I—"

"Because I'm partial to this lady downtown," he said. "I think she's on Jane Street."

"I wouldn't go to her," Patricia barked as she tried to wriggle the boning around her ribs loose. "She's so old and strange. Gives me the creeps."

Carrie picked up a pair of mustard-colored stockings from a cluttered worktable and handed them to Marlo. "Here. I believe these belong to you, my boy."

"Thank you, Car." He bent down and began rolling them onto his legs. "Don't listen to her. This one might be old, but she's good."

"Good at coughing all over her customers." Patricia tried to laugh, but the corset was too tight. "Really, Carrie, she's ancient. I wouldn't be surprised if she died in the middle of your meeting. Actually, she might already be dead she's so old."

"Trish!" Carrie scolded.

"Sorry. But it's true." She pointed to the lacing on her back and grimaced.

Carrie turned her head.

Marlo stood up, finally clothed. "Why are you looking for someone anyway? Need advice in love?" He smirked and tried to nudge her with his elbow.

She backed away. "No matter."

"But it does matter," he insisted. "Some are mediums. Some read the zodiac. Others can see the future. You need to know what you're looking for so you can pick the right person to see."

Carrie grimaced. She found a long piece of velvet and began to arbitrarily fold it. "I'm looking into a..." Her folding was becoming sloppy. "There may be a spirit that needs taking care of."

Marlo's face lit up. "Are you being haunted?"

"That is incredible," Patricia said in a whimper.

Carrie huffed and went to her. "That sounds silly." She yanked on a string, finally allowing the corset to expand.

Patricia audibly exhaled. "Thank you."

Carrie crossed her arms and stared at the floor. "I'm at my wits' end." Patricia and Marlo stood silently. She seemed as if she might begin to cry.

Finally, Marlo asked, "Do you know the ghost?"

"Yes," Carrie said before a sniffle. "It's my sister."

❖

"How did you hear about me?" Elisabeth asked with a slight German accent. She stood in the doorway like a tall spindly birch between Carrie and her apartment. Her pale blond hair was pulled into a tight bun that tightened the skin around her eyes. Her mouth, however, was extremely wrinkled. Lip stain seeped into the deep ridges, as if she had just eaten a beetroot like one would eat an apple. The rest of her face was unadorned. Her piercing blue eyes were makeup enough.

"From a friend," Carrie said. Her voice was dry and wobbly. "Patricia Winston is her name. She said you could"— she looked at Margarite standing beside her and decided to lean into Elisabeth's ear—"speak to the deceased."

Elisabeth laughed exactly three times, then smiled. "I can. The three of you may come in now."

Carrie's eyes seemed as if they might jump out of her skull. "It's just me and the girl."

Elisabeth stood to the side and gestured for them to enter. "So you think."

They settled onto a small couch across from a tall chair that Elisabeth sat stiffly into. Carrie declined her offer of tea even though she was thirsty for some. She wasn't too keen on consuming anything from that woman's kitchen. After all, it could be laced with herbs to make her services appear more impressive. Carrie had done her research.

"So, does the child know why you are here?" asked Elisabeth. She looked at Margarite even though she was addressing Carrie.

"You're a nurse," Margarite said. She played with a crocheted blanket draped over the arm on the sofa.

Carrie was quick to cut in. "Yes, I told her we are coming to see you because I fear she is ill."

"How long have you been deceased?" Elisabeth asked. She was looking at the spot next to Margarite.

Carrie perked up. "I beg your pardon?"

"Not you, the other woman."

She peered around, but nobody was in the room with them.

"You should have seen me sooner. You must cross over."

"What is she talking about, Mum?" Margarite asked. Her eyes began to swell with tears. She held the blanket in a tight fist.

"Please!" Carrie leaned forward. "What are you doing?"

Elisabeth whipped her head sharply in Carrie's direction. "You came here seeking help. You're haunted, yes?"

Carrie glanced at her niece, unable to decide if she should be so blunt in front of her.

"There's no use hiding the truth from the girl," said Elisabeth. "She has Sight. Must acknowledge it sooner than later, or I daresay she'll be shipped to a home for the insane." She focused on Margarite. "Child, the woman sitting next to you is your mother, yes?"

She nodded.

"Your mother, she is passed."

Margarite unhinged her jaw, not seeming to understand.

"She's dead, girl."

She turned her little head to the empty spot and transformed into a waterfall of tears.

Elisabeth placed a hand on her forehead and sighed. Then she leaned in to speak. "You must tell your daughter. She doesn't realize. It isn't fair to someone like her to have you here."

Carrie watched her niece lean into the air and give a muffled cry. Then the blanket lifted from the couch and draped itself onto Margarite's shoulders. Carrie stood and shrieked. "I demand to know what is happening!"

Elisabeth rose as well. "Your sister. She died on the journey here."

"I know. I have known. But why doesn't Margarite?"

"She can see the dead. She's been unaware of her mother's state. She'd have known the truth if everybody wasn't so afraid to speak about her passing." She looked at Margarite being cradled by what looked like nothing. "And if this ghost weren't so stubborn."

Carrie watched as Elisabeth bickered with the ghost of

her sister. She couldn't see her or hear her, but Elisabeth was reacting as anyone would react when having an argument. Very quickly, it became too much for Carrie, and the corners of the room darkened. Blackness crawled across her vision until she collapsed.

❖

The world was a blur as Carrie opened her eyes. For an instant, she believed herself to be home in bed, but as her vision adjusted, she noticed the light was different. A panic rose in her chest. She raised her head to see where she was.

"Oh, no," said Elisabeth. "Not so fast." She put her hands on Carrie's shoulders and gently coaxed her back to the pillow.

"I must have fainted," Carrie said. She squinted. Her head felt heavy, like after a night at the pub.

"Not must have. You did," said Elisabeth. She wrung a washcloth into a bowl and dabbed Carrie's face. "I apologize for that display. I often forget not everybody understands what I do."

Memories slammed back into Carrie's head with such strength, she sat up abruptly, almost knocking Elisabeth to the floor. "Margarite. Where is she?"

Elisabeth laid a hand on her shoulder and gently made her rest back into the couch again. "She is fine. Looking at cartoons in the kitchen."

Carrie's eyes glazed over. "And where is my sister?" Her voice quivered.

"She is gone. I made sure of it. Here, drink this." She held a teacup to Carrie's lips. Carrie sipped from it and then made a face of disgust. "I know it tastes terrible. It's a tonic to relax you."

Immediately, the mixture dulled the sharp edges of

Carrie's thoughts. "Are you a witch?" she asked. Her speech was slurred.

Elisabeth nodded. "I specialize in communication with spirits. It is the most common supernatural ability for humans to have. Like me, Margarite also has the Paramount of Sight."

Carrie stared at the ceiling for several seconds and wished, very genuinely, that she was the dead one, not her sister. After all she'd been through—the lost love, the starting over in a new country, the loneliness of growing old—why was she also given this to deal with? She felt as if the world was conspiring against her. What sin had she committed to deserve such adversity? "What will I do?" she cried. Then she corrected herself, "With her. What will I do with her?"

"She must learn to use her abilities for good. As the Way intended."

"How will she do that?" Carrie grunted. "From that cartoon strip? Or will there be a class held at the church?"

"Neither. She's looking at *Little Nemo in Slumberland*. That should only teach her to dream. And there are no formal classes for what she must study. Not here at least." Elisabeth sucked on her lips as she thought. "But I can teach her."

"You?"

"It is my duty. I have never had a ward. It is time."

Carrie looked around the room. That witch had nice things. Probably had quite the business bringing people in and speaking for the dead. She reached into her pocket. "What do I owe you for today?"

Elisabeth gasped. "Nothing. For you…for *her*, nothing. I would only gain from educating her. After years of false hopes in people only wishing or pretending to be gifted, she is real."

Carrie pondered the idea and hummed. "What will you teach her? To speak to the dead? She can already do that."

"There is more. There are ways to speak to them effectively. She must learn rules and stories and processes."

"And spells? Potions?"

Elisabeth was getting tangled for words. "Yes. If she has the ability and interest. If not, no."

"How did you get rid of my sister? How did you convince her to move on?"

The witch bit her lip and breathed. "I simply told her why she must move on. And I told her how."

"But she had reservations. That's why she haunted our wake, right?"

"She…"

Carrie leaned close to her and hissed, "Tell me."

"She was afraid of you raising her daughter. She was fearful you would resent Margarite."

Carrie's lip trembled. "I thought so." She stood and smoothed her clothing as she walked to the kitchen. Margarite was doing exactly what Elisabeth had said she was doing. "Girl, we need to go."

Margarite jumped to her feet. "This picture is so pretty, Auntie." She held a copy of the *New York Herald* high. "Can you read the *Nemo* story to me?"

"We will stop at the store and get our own copy."

"No," Elisabeth said. "She can borrow mine. I'll write my address on it so she can bring it to me one day." She stared at Carrie as if to ensure she understood the seriousness of the girl returning for lessons. Then she took the paper and scribbled a note below the comic.

Margarite's face was one giant smile. She launched herself into Elisabeth's breast for a hug.

"Thank you, Ms. Elisabeth," interrupted Carrie. "We'll be on our way." She held out her hand for Margarite.

"Please be in touch," Elisabeth whispered.

Carrie simply nodded, then yanked on her niece's arm as she went out the door.

❖

Once they were home and Margarite was in bed, Carrie turned to the last page and read Elisabeth's note. Her throat became tight with the beginnings of a sob. She quickly transformed that sadness into a growl as she tore the page away.

She'd raise the girl herself.

CLARISSA

Summer 1922

Clarissa recognized the new girl but couldn't recall from where. She was about her height, but shaped like a daisy: lithe, flat, and slightly frayed. Clarissa was more of a rose: curvy and soft in all the right places, also prickly. She figured they were about the same age. Maybe a year or two younger. Seventeen. Maybe eighteen. Her hair was black, but not the kind from a bottle like all the girls were wearing nowadays. It was a natural darkness. Like those Italians she often saw running around downtown. Or a Jew. But her nose wasn't strong enough. It was faint, just like her breasts.

Clarissa looked down at her own chest and smiled. She definitely had the new girl beat in that department.

Then she discreetly tightened her brassiere strap and smoothed her own naturally dark hair. If only her locks were as effortlessly silky as the new girl's. She paused. Clarissa had, until then, been the only girl with black hair on that stage. Another raven head in the troupe made her nervous. Their cast mates would compare their textures. The truth would be discovered. The *Weinstein Wonderacts'* dark secret would be revealed.

Stop, Clarissa. She collected her wits and decided to distract them with her approach. As she walked, she made sure to seem light on her feet, like her training had taught her, but heavy in the movement of her hips. She didn't learn that part in dance class.

"I see she has already made a flock of friends," Clarissa declared. She crossed her arms, then brought one hand to her chin. She traced her jaw with her index finger and half-smiled. The group of chorines that surrounded the new girl parted. The shuffling of their tap shoes across the worn wooden floor of that rehearsal room sounded like the squawking of strange tin birds as they flew from one tree to another. Clarissa now had a perfect view of her. She silently confirmed that the observations she'd made several feet back were correct. *A daisy, indeed.*

The new girl extended her hand. "You must be Clarissa Jenkins," she said. "I've read a lot about you, Ms. Jenkins."

Clarissa didn't budge. "Of course I'm Clarissa. I'm the only girl with black hair on the chorus line. Makes me stand out. We will have to lighten your curls as not to interfere."

The new girl's face went so pale it seemed like she might be sick.

Clarissa's stony expression cracked, and she allowed a slight, menacing smile to peek through. "Honey, I'm just giving you a hard time. I'm not that bristly." She finally unfolded her hand for a greeting. "I didn't get your name."

The new girl blinked twice and blew an uncomfortable laugh through her nose. "I'm sorry. My name is Margarite."

"Good to meet you, chickadee." She peered at the

others and then back to Margarite. "You know these fools or something?"

One of the male dancers stepped forward. "You *must* know Margarite."

Clarissa raised an eyebrow. "Frankie Warren, if I'd've known the girl, I wouldn't have introduced myself like a big dummy."

Frankie guffawed. "She's been around for ages. Took dancing class with most of us since we've been kids." He put a hand on Margarite's shoulder. "We're glad she finally got cast in something, isn't that right?" Everyone agreed with goofy smiles and nods.

"Well, Miss Margarite," Clarissa said as she re-crossed her arms. "These people here forget that I'm not from here. Everything I learned I learned from *my* people in *my* town. Which isn't this place."

She turned sharply on her heels and sauntered away. As she departed, she heard Frankie say, "Don't worry. She's like that with *everyone*."

❖

"I like this place better, anyhow," Salvatore said. Clarissa could tell he was being genuine because he was smiling *and* raising his eyebrows. From him, one or the other was bad news, but both meant something good. His face was like a child's in that respect. When he was happy, you could read him like a billboard in Times Square.

Still, she felt self-conscious about taking him to Jackson's. Sal usually visited places like Connie's on 131st, a whites-only club that featured almost exclusively black performers. She knew he wasn't a fan of the segregation between stage and table, but the talent Connie's brought in was too good for a man like him to shy away from. But because she was nervous about their door policy, a mixed club like Jackson's was the next best thing.

"I'm excited to see what this place offers. Do you know any of the performers tonight?" he asked.

"Maybe when I see them onstage I'll recognize one or two," she said. She smoothed a giant curl to her cheek. "Lord knows they won't be as masterful as what you're used to several blocks south. They've taken most of the good acts."

He gave her a mournful look, then continued to scan the crowd. "Quite a turnout they've got here." He became very serious. "Do they have a second exit?"

She pointed to the door of an *out of order* ladies room. "It's been 'broken' since they opened. It's hard to fix a bathroom that's actually a stairwell to the street." She winked.

"Ever been raided?"

She fluttered her lashes in a blasé manner. "Probably. Never on a night I've been here." She pushed him into a seat at a small table near the stage. "Try the punch. In addition to several *secret* ingredients, it's got pineapple in it."

Sal smiled and picked up a menu. She was glad he didn't seem to be scrutinizing how unglamorous Jackson's was. They didn't have linen on the tables, and the basement it was located in looked just like...well, a basement. Many of the other speakeasies in town tried to dress themselves up, but Jackson's didn't focus much on presentation. All the owners cared about was people gathering for a few drinks, a few songs, and a few hours away from reality.

At the table next to them, two men howled at a joke their waiter had told. Then one of the men put a hand on the other's shoulder. He didn't pat his companion like most men would, he squeezed him. Affectionately.

"I see several of *my people* are here," Sal sang. "That's good."

Clarissa covered a laugh under bright red fingernails. "Your people? You mean rehearsal pianists?"

"Oh, yes. Yes, of course!"

They shared a silent giggle, then Clarissa reached out for his hand. "You should come here with Vincent, darling."

"I think you're more likely to see a cop walk in and order gin before he risks coming to a place like this." He raised his hand to signal a waiter.

Clarissa unintentionally let a frown show.

"No, no...not like that," he said, scooting his chair closer to hers. "This place is great. I'm glad you've brought me. You know what I'm talking about. He's got an image to preserve."

"I know. People like riffraff until they're sharing a dance floor with them. One may only enjoy Negroes and *homosexuals* from afar." She sat up straight, rolled her shoulders, and secured her purse on her lap. "That's why I'm dancing at the end of the chorus line, where I can move too quickly for anyone to notice what color I really am." She winked again.

"You know I don't like that kind of talk, Clar."

"Well, I don't like having to pretend to be a white woman to be on a Broadway stage."

"You *are* a white woman."

"I'm a black woman, too." Clarissa realized she was speaking too forcefully. She lowered her voice. "Or as you all like to say, a Sicilian. How exotic." She raised her hand and snapped, demanding the attention of a waiter.

Sal wriggled uncomfortably in his seat. "While we're talking about the end of the chorus line..."

"What? Have they designed something new for me to wear?" She struck a pose.

He picked at a splinter in the center of the table. "I don't know if this will be appealing to you or not, but..."

"Salvatore, say it or I'll knock it outta you, I will." She pointed her index finger inches from the end of his nose.

He stared at it cross-eyed for a moment, then exhaled the news. "They want the new girl to be at the end."

Clarissa sat still and blinked twice. "Who? Mildred?"

"It's Margarite."

"Same thing." She chewed on the inside her cheek as she let the idea brew. Then she exploded, "So I'm done. Gotta go to Sixty-Third Street and dance with all the other Negros in *Shuffle Along*? Or should I look for work in some vaudeville tent traveling around Missouri or something?"

"Relax," he said sternly. "Don't be ridiculous. You're not done. You're just getting a new act."

"Fantastic. Going to have me embrace my mother's side by corking my face, slapping a rag on my head and singing about 'missin' ma colafoo man'? Or maybe I can tap across the stage in front of giant slices of watermelon like the colored girls do in *The Bridgeport Blackbirds*."

"It won't be like those shows, Clar. I don't know what the new bit is. I just know they—"

"Don't want me in the white act. I know." She crossed her arms and looked off to another part of the crowded room. "Where the hell is that waiter?"

"I told them you wouldn't be happy."

"They don't care if I'm happy or not," she snapped. "They just care if I'm selling tickets. Well, let me tell you, I've been getting thunderous applause every night. *Every night!*"

"You don't have to tell me. I'm there. I know. But having you dance next to all those white girls, it's risky. It makes Weinstein nervous. You're better off in your own number, where you can't be compared to anyone else. Believe me, it's for the best."

"What's for the best?" squeaked a voice from behind her.

Clarissa turned. The last person she wanted to see, Margarite, was standing behind her with Frankie and two other girls from the line. Their big smiles turned serious when they saw Clarissa's swollen eyes.

"I'm sorry, were we interrupting something?" asked Frankie. He started to push the girls to another table.

"No, no. It's fine. I'm happy to see you all!" Clarissa exclaimed through a thick layer of faux excitement. "Salvatore here was just telling me about the updates being made in the show." She raised her voice an octave. "I'm getting my own number."

Frankie and the girls squealed with delight. The other patrons turned and stared. They huddled together and giggled with embarrassment from their outburst.

"That's really something, Miss Jenkins," said Margarite. She laid a hand on her shoulder.

Clarissa shivered from her touch. "Please." She spoke through gritted teeth. "Do call me Clarissa." She dryly swallowed some anger and changed the subject. "I didn't know you were a fan of Jackson's."

"I've never been. But these folks wanted to take me out to celebrate being in the show. I'm glad to run into you here."

"I'll give you one more thing to celebrate."

Sal reached over and placed a hand on her arm. "Clarissa."

"Oh, Sal. She ought to know. It's good news." She turned to Margarite. "You're dancing at the end of the line."

A giant grin stretched across Margarite's face. Her tiny lips seemed to disappear into the smile. Then her eyes widened with a thought. She became serious. "But you dance there."

"I *did*," Clarissa said sharply. Everyone nearby jerked to attention. "But as you overheard Sal saying, it's for the best."

Margarite looked to the others for help, but they were staring uncomfortably at the floor. "I don't understand. You're perfectly lovely at the end of the line."

"Thank you, dear. And you're right. I am lovely. But the girl at the end of the chorus line should be *funny*. She starts off the show a mess. She goofs up the steps, can't keep rhythm, trips over her own two feet. A riot. But I'm better suited somewhere else." She glared at Salvatore. "Somewhere in the show where my specifically *ethnic* looks can be appreciated on their own." She stood to look Margarite straight in the face. "Better to have someone like you, what with your long limbs and big goofy eyes. You'll be funny. You'll be perfect."

A drum roll split the tension and a tall man in tails walked on the stage. "And now, pleasant patrons of Jackson's House, I am pleased to present to you the stunning, the marvelous, that siren of song and dance, Miss Clarissa Jenkins!"

Every person in the room turned to Clarissa. As the applause swelled, she kept her focus on Margarite. She raised her eyebrows, pouted her lips, then she walked up the small stairs to the stage. Several lights illuminated her face, making the tiny rhinestones pinned in her curls twinkle like a marquee. As the clapping subsided, she pointed to a waiter walking by. "Hey, mister. I've been trying to get a punch since I stepped foot in this hole. Bring one here before I get too parched to hit my high notes."

The crowd laughed. Margarite tried to participate, but the tremor in her lips made it impossible to smile.

❖

The first day of rehearsal on the stage after sets had been installed was always thrilling. Even for those who shielded their emotions, like Clarissa, the awe of performing in a masterpiece of a building like the Duchess Theatre was hard to contain. "You'd have thunk this was my debut season in the show the way I'm smiling," she said to Sal as they walked through the wings into the cavernous space. A single light bulb on a stand was wheeled in the middle of the stage, causing their shadows to stretch to gargantuan lengths across the audience.

"Golly," said Margarite when she stepped onstage. Her voice echoed abrasively through the fly space above them.

Clarissa shuddered. Even though rehearsals had been going on for weeks, she still couldn't find a place in her heart for that girl. Everything about her was irritating. At first, she'd been annoyed by her shyness and formality, addressing everyone as *miss* and *sir* when she'd probably known them long enough to be on a first-name basis. Then, once she'd settled into friendships with other cast members, her meek voice boomed and her limbs loosely jingled like all the other flappers slinking up Fifth Avenue. Her style of dancing was just as fluttery. That modulation of proper technique wasn't Clarissa's taste. The same went for her singing. No classic soprano or alto training there, but a sort of loud speaking in tune. That and the elasticity of her face forced every performance of hers to wander into comedic territory. Clarissa yearned for reviews to expose her as a one-note funny girl.

A handful of other actors trickled onstage. Frankie ran up to the light stand and danced a circle around it. "Do you think these things really work?" he asked with a ghoulish affectation.

"It obviously works," said Margarite. "It's on, isn't it?"

"For the spirits." He spoke to her as if she was a child.

Margarite raised an eyebrow.

"It's a ghost lamp."

Her face reddened. "I thought it was just a light left burning so we could find our way in before the house lights come on."

"Nope." He tiptoed toward her and spoke with Shakespearean exaggeration. "We keep this lamp ablaze so the ghosts of the theater have an opportunity to perform by it when we leave at night." He twiddled his fingers in her face in an attempt to frighten her. "That way they won't curse our production."

Clarissa narrowed her eyes at him. "Frankie, have some respect."

"For what? We aren't in a cemetery."

"You don't know what happened in this place before you got here. This theater is almost as old as you."

"Well, it just seems like a waste to leave a light burning if there aren't confirmed ghosts in here."

Sal and Clarissa didn't comment, just exchanged silent glances and smirked.

"What's that about?" Frankie asked.

"I don't know what you're talking about," said Clarissa.

"I saw that look. Is there a ghost here?"

Sal stepped forward. "There are ghosts in every theater. Everyone knows that." He grabbed the light stand.

Frankie laughed. "Marg, you don't believe any of this hooey, do you?"

Margarite tightened her lips and glanced at the floor.

"I don't believe it. A superstitious bunch I'm with, hey?"

"No," she finally said. "I just don't like the nickname Marg. It's ugly."

"Fine." Frankie looked at the three of them. "I gotta piss. If I'm not back in ten minutes, Hamlet's daddy got me." He disappeared into the shadows backstage.

Salvatore groaned and rolled his head, cracking his neck

twice. "Margarite, you weren't all wrong. This does give us light to find switches, too. So I'm going to take this and get the place bright enough to rehearse in." The casters were old, so the whole contraption wobbled as it made its way across the stage. The two women were momentarily left alone. They'd have to make small talk, something Clarissa despised doing with anyone, let alone *her*. Instead of interacting with Margarite, she watched the light bounce away into the wings. She hoped Margarite was doing the same.

When Sal and his lamp were about three feet from disappearing behind the proscenium arch, the wheel hit a snag. The light jerked and briefly went out. In that second of blackness, Margarite gasped and clutched Clarissa's forearm.

When the light came back on, they were looking at each other. Before that moment, Clarissa would have violently snatched her arm out of that girl's grasp and berated her for invading her personal space. But the look on Margarite's face changed her mind. She was pale as paper. Her eyes were black, her pupils dilated to the very edge of her blue irises. Something seemed to have frightened her. Clarissa's heart leapt to her throat.

Margarite caught herself hanging on to her co-star. "I'm sorry, Clarissa."

"You see something?"

Her mouth tightened again.

Clarissa's voice was intense and quiet. "People don't just go grabbing one another."

"I thought I saw someone," she whispered.

"Maybe you did. We're scheduled to start soon. Could have been another dancer."

Suddenly the stage door flew open, flooding the stage with sunlight from the street. Several more performers sauntered in, loud, excited, and ready to begin.

❖

The next two weeks of rehearsing onstage with costumes and sets went by swiftly, as most tasks do when a deadline looms. But unlike most deadlines, opening night wasn't ominous. It was quite the opposite; a glittering ball of excitement, flashing bulbs, and applause awaited the cast at the end of their tunnel. This 1922 season of *Weinstein's Wonderacts* was the talk of the town. The storybook set pieces and elaborately costumed showgirls were always exciting, but it was the array of characters onstage that really had ticket holders ready to tear down the door.

Vincent Croft was headlining the spectacle. His good looks, charm, and singing voice had made quite a splash in the 1920 edition. Audiences couldn't get enough, and the producers were forced to add number after number featuring him front and center. It only made sense to put his name in lights right above the title.

Where Vincent Croft was, Madelyn Vicks was never far behind. Their duets were so popular, it was hardly imaginable he could sing with anyone but her. He was the constant charmer, and she played hard to get. At the beginning of their songs, they were typically argumentative and flirtatious, but by the bridge they'd always fall for each other. This new revue promised two show-stopping numbers featuring them and a chorus of thirty dancing girls in costumes with, as the advertisements put it, "more sparkle than the crown jewels!" And because the show's director and producer, Ernst Weinstein, wanted as much press as possible, the two extended their romance into real life. Seeing them walk down the street or cuddling in a corner booth at a restaurant was as useful as any billboard. The public was nuts for them.

The darling couple was accompanied by an array of funny men and women, including Bigs Spencer, a large black man who was famous for his pantomime of an overly hungry party guest. His presence in an otherwise all-white show was a controversy that caused ticket sales to soar. Weinstein hired Clarissa with hopes two black performers would bring in two times the cash. Unfortunately, he grew timid. One black performer was novelty, but two could look political. Clarissa was too talented for him to let her go, so he had her skin powdered and her hair smoothed. Clarissa Jenkins became an exotic beauty, one he'd present dripping in gold and encrusted with gems. Dancers tapped around her wearing loincloths and animal masks while a three-story pyramid rose from upstage. Her version of Cleopatra hit the highest notes on Broadway and was destined to be a hit.

"The crowd is going to go absolutely wild during this number," Sal said after they'd run through it. He stood up in the orchestra pit and reached for her hand.

Clarissa twiddled her fingers with his and grinned. "Do you really think so?" she panted, trying to catch her breath from the aggressive dance routine.

"Absolutely. Not so mad about getting moved to a new slot now, are you?"

Ernst Weinstein stood up. "We'll see when the reviews come out," he said. He walked down the aisle to the stage. He motioned for her to lean down so he could speak softly. "This is a more appropriate bit for you, I think. Really captures the opulence of the Nile. You really capture why Cleopatra's reign was so triumphant." He looked at her and winked. "You were great, kid."

Clarissa didn't bother correcting his inaccuracy; she just accepted his compliment and left the stage. Mr. Weinstein was a notoriously cantankerous man. He loved and hated in extremes, and those feelings were never fixed. One day he'd have a favorite number, and the next day it'd be out of the show because he overheard two old women complain about it at intermission. *Weinstein's Wonderacts* was always evolving. Everybody involved tried their best to stay in the show by keeping on his good side. Clarissa was especially cautious because her presence on that stage was already controversial, so she accepted every note he threw at her.

When she walked into the wings, she tore the headdress off, shook out her hair, and fanned herself with her hand. "It's warm back here, isn't it? I'm looking forward to autumn." She saw Eva, one of the dancers, in the stairwell drinking a tall glass of water. Condensation dribbled down the glass and on to her hand. Clarissa smacked her lips. She had a pitcher in her dressing room, but it was up several flights of stairs. "Eva, darling, where'd you get that?"

Eva hastily finished swallowing and exhaled. "From Charlie, the new stagehand. He's got a bucket of it around here somewhere." Just then a square man with thinning hair lumbered up to her. She handed him the glass and put her hand on his shoulder. "Here he is. Have you met?"

Clarissa shook her head.

"This is Charlie. Charlie, this is Clarissa. She's a fabulous dancer."

Clarissa dipped into a slight curtsy and smiled. "Good to meet you, Charlie. You don't have another one of those glasses floating around, do you?"

Charlie rolled Eva's hand from his shoulder and stepped forward. He stared into Clarissa's eyes. "No," he said. His voice was deep and cold. "Afraid I don't." Then he turned and shoved his way through a mess of curtains.

The blood rushed from Clarissa's limbs and settled in her head. She was warmer than before, but not from heat. She simmered with silent rage under her powdered face. She'd known men like that before. There'd been tons of them back home in Louisiana. They looked at her like she was something they'd throw in the trash if it weren't for onlookers. They possessed the same gruff voice and rigid demeanor. They denied her things that were available to others.

She stormed up the stairs with eyes open wider than Grand Central Station. She let the rush of air dry the tears that threatened to spill over her lashes. No way would she let others see her even the slightest bit down. She'd faced adversity almost all her life, but this was too close. That theater was her home, and he was polluting it. She became so lost in thought she barged right into another girl running down the stairs.

"Clarissa, you startled me." It was Margarite.

It was her own fault for being so distracted, but Clarissa played it off like it wasn't. "What're you in such a rush for? You have three numbers before you need to be out there."

Margarite held up a yellow sequined strap. "This came loose from my dress. If I don't get it fixed, I'm afraid I'll come tumbling out." She made a goofy face and laughed that small walrus laugh Clarissa hated.

"Oh, honey." Clarissa chuckled. "You don't have enough to go tumblin'. They'd simply just *slip* out." She slithered to her left to move past her.

Margarite slid with her, blocking the way. "I'm sorry you're still sore about me taking the role. But what was I supposed to do? Turn it down? This job is my dream."

"I'm not aching in the least. I got a number. Hell, I even have a pyramid. I'm fine." She attempted to squeeze between the railing and her body.

"You're upset."

"I told you, I'm not."

"No. About something else. Your eyes are red." Clarissa

elbowed her way through and got up one stair before Margarite caught her arm. "Are you all right? He keeps asking me."

Clarissa's hair stood on end. That hot feeling came back to her face. "Who? That Charlie character?"

Margarite wrinkled her nose. "Lord, no. I don't talk to him. He rubs me all kinds of wrong."

Clarissa's heart settled. Good, she wasn't the only one.

"That other guy. The tall one with the reddish beard. He keeps wondering if you're all right. Asks me to tell you to be well."

Clarissa's face dropped. She let out a tiny moan. "What are you talking about?"

"The stagehand." Margarite raised both eyebrows. "He's very nice. Kind of peculiar. I think he said his name is Douglas."

"Dacey."

"I'm sorry?"

"Douglas Dacey."

"That's right. He a friend of yours?"

Clarissa stared at the wall behind her for a moment, and then blinked back to reality. "Excuse me. I need to get to my room. I'm very thirsty." She turned and pulled herself up the remaining stairs, stopping on the landing. "Tell him not to worry. If you see him."

When she finally arrived to her tiny dressing room, the queen of the Nile closed the door tightly behind her and cried.

❖

Harold rolled over to retrieve a cigarette from the case in his pants pocket. They'd been ripped off and left on the floor by the bed. He clumsily opened the silver container and stuck a cigarette between his teeth, smiling at her. Clarissa liked his smile, even with a smoke in the middle of it. Then he returned to rummaging, now through the bedside table for a book of matches. "I know there's gotta be lights in here."

"I can page the front desk," Clarissa said. She smirked. "They can't tell my color over the phone."

"They can't tell your color in real life, either." Harold's eyes widened. "Aha!" He removed a match from the carton and lit the cigarette. The cherry burned orange, illuminating his face in strange light.

Clarissa gazed at the bright wallpaper and the polished walnut armoire. "My mama would fall over dead if she knew her girl was staying in a room at the Plaza." She balled up the sheets near her clavicle and crawled into the nook under his arm. "She'd never believe they didn't make me walk through the kitchen to get here, either."

"You're a star, though." He blew smoke into the air. "Of course you're here."

She laughed, just once. It was a sarcastic, gruff sound. "If I didn't know you, I'd call you ignorant. But you're really just kind." She raised her hand and extended two fingers. "Give me some of that, Mr. Roth." As she inhaled the burnt-chocolatey smoke, she ran her free hand down the sheets. They were softer than anything she'd known. Then she bolted out of bed and ran to the heavy curtains. She threw them to one side and allowed the last few minutes of sunlight to permeate the room.

Harold shielded his eyes even though the light coming in was too weak to be even remotely startling.

"Don't be a baby, darling. Girls like me don't get to enjoy views like this every day, you know." Being out of those sweaty sheets felt nice on her skin. She glanced back at the room and realized she was probably backlit from the setting sun. She rested one hand on her hip and brought the cigarette to her lips seductively with the other. Clarissa was very aware of how tantalizing she appeared silhouetted in that window.

Harold threw the sheets to his feet and lay on his side. He was aroused again. "I think you've put a spell on me."

"If you're making a voodoo joke, I'm gonna knock you upside the head." They shared a laugh. She liked making him laugh, forcing out more and more of those smiles she loved. He was older than her, probably by ten years, and seeing him smile made him appear more youthful. His laugh lines were marks of pure happiness instead of age. When he wasn't chuckling, the stress scratched notches near his eyes and forehead, a tally of the worries on his mind.

"I'm excited for the show to open next week," he said.

"You just want to see me shake my derrière." She sauntered back to the bed. "Well, Mr. Roth, I can do that for you any day." She jumped onto him and fiendishly kissed his chest.

"Watch out for the smoke."

"I'm careful," she said, muffled into his skin. Her right arm was extended high above them, the cigarette safely burning away from flesh.

"And stop calling me Mr. Roth." He held her still, forcing her to look at him. "I'm Harold. You can call me Harold."

"You're no fun." She rolled off him on the other side of the large bed. "I like being reminded that I'm screwing the show's investor."

"Is that all I am to you, Miss Jenkins?"

"No, baby," she purred, dropped the cigarette in a glass of water, and brushed away a curl on his forehead. "You're nice. You treat me real well."

"I don't know how anyone could treat you wrong." He

inhaled deeply, then exhaled the words "so beautiful" with intensity.

Clarissa skipped a beat and sat up. "Remember that stagehand? The one I told you about? The real nice one. Douglas."

Harold seemed confused. "I believe. The one who helped you that one night."

"Yes, him. Well, we have this new broad in the show. Dancing at the end of the line."

"Weinstein told me about her. Supposed to be a riot."

"Debatable. Anyhow, she got me in a corner the other day. Chattering like a squirrel, and I'm trying to make an entrance. Said Douglas *spoke* to her."

Harold slowly elevated his back to put his head at the same level as hers. "Please, go on."

"Not much else, I'm afraid." She rolled her fingers along the sheets and lowered her eyes to her knee. "Said he kept asking if I was doing well." When she looked back at him, she blinked out a single tear stained black from her eye makeup. "She told me like nothing about it was strange, like it was completely ordinary."

He was stroking her arm by this point, trying to be comforting. "Well, did you tell her?"

She shook her head.

"It's clear she doesn't know. She doesn't realize the circumstances." He stopped rubbing her arm. "But this is good."

Clarissa wrinkled her face and pulled away. "Pardon?"

"This girl, she'll be at the party this weekend?"

"I suppose. Everyone loves her."

He stared off into nowhere and smiled. "She'll get to meet everyone."

"She knows everyone. She's in the godforsaken show. Are you all right?"

He rubbed her shoulders and looked into her eyes. "I mean she'll meet *everyone*. And in a new way. This girl could be a fine addition to the Circle."

Clarissa didn't like talking about other women in bed. But he had a point. Margarite might fit in after all.

MARGARITE

Summer 1922

Before she met Frankie at the train station, Margarite primped at home. She combed her hair *just so* before adding the hat. When she placed it on her head, she decided the angle wasn't right. She moved it. An unruly hair sprung up. "Damn."

New approach: put the hat on first, find the perfect degree for it to tilt, and *then* finish her hair.

Hmm. But that would mean when she took the hat off at the party, her hair'd be a mess underneath. She cursed the waves she'd been born with. They were her mother's curls. "You had them too, Aunt Carrie," she said.

The room was still. Margarite paused for total silence. She even held her breath. She waited for a breeze, a creak, a knock—anything. The only noise came from the street below.

She scooted her chair away from the mirror with a thoughtlessness that would have made Carrie holler about scratching the wooden floors, and she walked into the other room. Her heels clunked on the boards. "If you were still around, I'd have a better-fitting outfit." She yanked open a small drawer at the top of the dresser and pulled out a chipped green box. "I'm taking your necklace. It's not as long as what's in fashion nowadays, but it's pretty. Always looked nice on you." She halted and listened again. Nothing. "I'll try not to lose it." Still nothing. "Or maybe I will. I'll just throw it in Long Island Sound."

Her face became warm. "Where are you?" she yelled. "I'm supposed to be able to see you. Why aren't you here?"

Her ability to distinguish life from death was undeveloped. More often than not, the dead appeared to her like any other living person. For Margarite, there was no line between worlds. The ghosts weren't disfigured, bleeding, or mauled. She didn't see any transparency, glistening, or fog surrounding them. To her they appeared as real as her cast mates, as Miss Mabel across the hall.

She spent hours perusing obituaries, preparing for encounters. She had to be on the lookout for certain symptoms of death because the names didn't always come with photographs. These official qualities didn't come from any expert, she'd just noticed them through the years. Often she'd observe a person meandering down the street or mundanely performing a task, and she'd look at the face. It would seem sullen and dejected, eyes somewhere beyond the present. A person like that could be a ghost—a sad one either unaware or rejecting its lot. Or she'd spot someone racing through traffic with fearless determination, roaming through crowds examining every passerby, maybe calling a name. More often than not, that person was also dead, seeking to tie up loose ends or communicate to a loved one.

So even though she had no formal training, Margarite felt confident in her abilities to discern soul from flesh. At least most of the time. She'd been thrown off before. Moments like that disturbed her, made her question everything about what was real and what wasn't. Sometimes she wondered if everyone in her life was a ghost, that the entirety of existence was just in her head. The only person who knew about her curse was Aunt Carrie. Margarite could reach out to her when everything seemed confusing. Carrie could calm her, point out the real from the not. But now Carrie was dead. And she didn't even stick around to haunt her.

"I don't know why you didn't stay," Margarite sighed. "You could have. You knew I'd see you. We could still be together." A tear welled in the corner of her eye. She'd spent an hour doing her makeup and didn't have enough time to do it over again, so she sniffed it back and exhaled her sadness away. She had a party to get to.

❖

The train lumbered to the platform at the Port Washington station. It seemed to Margarite that the conductor couldn't find the proper speed to approach or the exact place to stop. After several jerks forward, the machinery screeched to a halt. Her oversized green hat flopped over her freshly sheared bangs. "Goddamn it," she said. She smiled to recover from her unladylike outburst and placed the hat back on top of her head. She dabbed her hair back in place with one spindly finger. "It took me forever to tame this mane."

Frankie stood up and helped her from the sticky leather seat. "Milady," he said, extending a hand. She took it and stood. "You look ravishing."

"So do you." She smiled and admired his sunny yellow shirt shining beneath a very smart gray suit.

"It's fun dressing up, isn't it? Honestly, these parties are the only time I ever do."

"How many of these things have you been to?"

He twisted his lips and thought. "I believe three. He

holds two a season. One in the summer and one in the winter. Something about where the moon is. You know, you're going to love it. I'm so glad you got invited." He grabbed her hands and squealed.

Margarite didn't share his glee. "I thought everyone in the cast got invited."

Frankie cackled. "That's a hysterical thought. The guest list is controlled by the Dark Lady and her band of Merry Men." He motioned for the road. "Cars are over there."

Margarite shook her head. She thought the world of Frankie but was irritated that he smacked pet names on everybody. "You mean Clarissa."

"And Sal and Vincent."

She could understand Vincent having a hand in the invites. He was the star of the show. She didn't know for sure how Sal fit in, but she'd heard gossip about them being lovers. Frankie's nickname, *merry men*, pretty much confirmed that. She felt a pang of sadness for Vincent's reported girl, Madelyn Vicks. Did she know about their affair? Anyway, Vincent and Sal made sense, but Clarissa? She was a name, but she was just in one number. Entertainers like her didn't throw parties on the Gold Coast. "Why would she…"

A car horn honked three times, and the chauffeur waved his hand from the driver's side of a gleaming blue car.

"That must be Jim!" Frankie said. His face lit up. "Roth's driver." He got about one inch from her face and looked her square in the eyes. "He's adorable." Frankie grabbed her hand and whisked her into the backseat of the car.

❖

The fountain outside Roth's mansion was splendid, more impressive than the ones Margarite had seen as a child at

Dreamland on Coney Island. The ones in the city were nice. Grand, classic, and made of stone. Nothing like Roth's, though. This one was all water, geyser after geyser shooting straight into the night sky and back down again. She stood beside it and breathed in the coolness emanating from its mists.

"Don't stand too close, you'll get soaked," Frankie said. He was already grabbing a glass of champagne from a waiter positioned at the front steps. He took another and held it out for her. "Come on in."

Two giant Gothic doors muffled the music and conversation until a pair of butlers turned the latches and swung them open, releasing the energy that pulsated from behind them. The party hit like a speeding streetcar. People were everywhere, dressed in the most glittering and luxurious array of ensembles Margarite had ever seen, almost more beautiful than the costumes in the show they were celebrating.

Under her feet was a rug woven from what seemed like a thousand colors and patterns. It stretched across the massive entryway until it met three steps that led to a sunken room with glass walls called Palm Court. The band was set up in there: a trio of instruments and a singer with platinum-blond hair. The hundreds of sequins on her dress reflected the hundreds of twinkling lights strung from the ceiling, creating a virtual lightning storm in the smoke-filled room. On the opposite side of the foyer was a grand staircase that spiraled three or four stories before meeting a stained glass dome in the ceiling.

"Holy hell," Margarite said. "People live like this?"

If Frankie hadn't snapped his fingers in front of her face, her tongue would have fallen out of her gaping mouth. "I'm going to see when Jim's done for the night. I'll find you later." He winked and strutted back out the doors.

Margarite stood by herself, only half in the party. Her dress was light sage, cut right below the knee and decorated with lace. She'd seen it in the window of some fancy store and only recently had the money to feel confident enough to even walk in and touch it. Being in the show had made it possible to do that and more. Now she owned it and felt like a million bucks. Well, until she looked at the pageantry surrounding her. Those gals made her look like she'd be more at home at an Easter luncheon. At least she had that hat to make her feel done-up. She was going to adjust it, but she'd left it in the car. "Damnit!" she said. She walked back outside hoping Jim hadn't driven away with it in the backseat.

Luckily the car was still there. Frankie leaned against it, wearing her hat.

"Hey, miss!" called Margarite. "I don't think green's your color." He stuck out his tongue at her. They shared a laugh that was soon interrupted by a roar, and she ran back inside.

Several shrieks came from deep within the party. "It's divine! What a beauty!" said Vincent Croft. He appeared seconds later, feigning shock from what he'd just seen. "Did you see the leopard?" he asked a cluster of pale ladies. "Roth-y got a leopard for us. I told him he should put it in the show." He scanned the crowd, shrugged, and yelled in no particular direction. "Hey, Roth-y, put that in the show!" He turned in Margarite's direction and twiddled his fingers at her. "You look ravishing, my dear. Kiss."

"Thank you." She studied his outfit: a long, sparkling black cape with Oriental detailing billowed behind him. A top hat finished the look. "And you look very dashing."

He threw his blond head backward and let out a cackle. "It's the only time we can dress so extravagantly." He looked her up and down. "You're dressed so prettily. Modest for this crowd. You're shy, aren't you?"

"I'm not shy," she said "You just never speak to me enough to know any different."

He glared at her for a split second, then grinned. "Here. Wear my cape. It'll jazz you right up." Vincent swung the cloak off his shoulders like a magician. He draped it over her and stood back to admire his creation. As he was about to speak, a waiter waltzed by with a tray and stole his attention. "Oh, have you tried this lamb? It's *divine*. Has a mint *goo* on it. Just very interesting. And *divine*."

The waiter held a silver tray for them to take a piece of miniature lamb chop. Margarite had trouble finding an opening in her new shroud to reach for one. The waiter obviously grew tired of waiting for her and floated away before she could manage.

Vincent chewed the meat and put three fingers over his mouth while he spoke. "You're coming upstairs with us later."

"For what?"

"Oh, you know."

She cocked her head and twisted her face. "No. I don't."

He mimicked her expression. "Clarissa led me to believe that's why you're here."

This was getting tedious. "I'm here because I'm in the show. With you."

For probably the first time in a long while, Vincent Croft's face turned red. "I know that, silly! But...but...you can be invited to the party," he said, waving around the room, "and then you can be invited to the *party*." He pointed upstairs.

Margarite huffed. "Mr. Croft, I just—"

"Vincent," he said. "Call me Vincent."

"Vincent, I really have no idea what you're talking about."

"Christ." He turned to a nearby gentleman, grabbed his coupe, and took a swig of champagne. "I thought Sal would have...where is he? Salvatore!" He handed the man back his glass and wandered several feet calling for Sal. By now he'd attracted an audience.

Sal rounded a corner, clutching a cocktail. "Vince, I'm right here," he said. "Foghorn."

Vincent smiled and kissed him quickly on the lips.

Sal's expression was panicked. "You're drunk," he said under his breath. "Be careful."

"Please, Salvatore." Vincent was practically screaming again. "Everyone here knows. It's the theater."

Sal looked around and grinned at Margarite. "You look lovely tonight."

"This place is a haven for the strange," continued Vincent. "And for leopards." He cackled again.

She stepped forward. "Vincent mentioned something about going upstairs. Does this involve *anything else* illegal? Because I don't know if I can handle more." She held up the coupe of champagne.

Vincent moved in and pretended to whisper. "Not one for the giggle water, are you?"

Margarite knew he was trying to make her blush, but she wouldn't allow herself to. "Not usually. It...um...clouds my judgment." The men chuckled, thinking she was referring to making a fool of herself, but she was actually talking about her ability to decipher the living from the dead. When her mind wasn't clear, neither were her instincts. A year prior, she indulged with some friends and ended up talking to a spirit in a corner for twenty-five minutes. They witnessed her speaking to the wall, but all the while Margarite thought she was conversing with a nice man from Yonkers that everybody could see. Those friends were not her friends anymore.

❖

Upstairs was a maze of rooms and hallways. Margarite found it hard to imagine why Mr. Roth, a bachelor, would need so much space. She came to the conclusion it was pride. He wasn't brought up in wealth. His parents were from a snowy village across the ocean. He was the first son born in the new world, and he somehow struck it rich. The house, with its Gothic arches, oriental rugs, and imported flora, was his way of communicating *I've made it.* And for Margarite, it worked. In that house, she saw all the hopes and dreams of the families in her crumbling tenement completely realized. If he could do it, people like them had potential. People like them could make it. Big.

"It's impressive," she said as she walked down a hallway with luxurious textured wallpaper. Her hand grazed velvet.

"He's quite an egg. It's a bit much if you ask me," said Sal. "It's almost grotesque." He escorted her by the arm to the secret party Vincent had spoke about earlier. All the other invitees had already gone up, but Sal and Margarite took their time. They wandered the halls slowly and observantly, like a pair of old ghosts.

Margarite was glad to have a moment alone with him. She always liked Sal, even if their interactions were limited to rehearsals around a piano. He was patient with her. Kind. After finally conversing with Vincent, she was surprised Sal was so close to a character like him. They were polar opposites in terms of demeanor. Clarissa, too. To Margarite, she seemed like one of the more uneven people on the planet. Kind one minute and a nightmare the next.

"You still haven't told me what this is," she said. She felt his arm tense.

"Margarite." He stopped. "We need your assistance with something."

She nodded, asking him to continue.

"Some of us from the cast…well, actually from the whole production, we socialize outside of the theater."

"That's wonderful. I do the same. With Frankie and—"

"Yes. I'm aware. And I'd appreciate if what I tell you, what you see tonight, is...um...hidden from them. Discretion is of the utmost importance." He shifted and closed his eyes. "To know. To dare. To will." He opened them and stared at her very seriously. "To keep silent."

As he spoke, Margarite found herself unintentionally holding her breath. The hair on her arms stood to attention.

"The code," he added.

"Of what?" She instinctually shifted her weight into her heels as if she might have to escape.

"Our Circle."

She made a queer, confused face.

"A coven."

Still, what he said wasn't registering.

He glanced both ways down the hallway. "Witches."

Margarite heard her own laugh before she realized she was doing so. The labyrinth of halls acted like a pipe organ that blasted her guffaws through the entire upstairs level. She gasped and slammed her hands against her mouth to muffle any lingering noise. "I'm so sorry, Sal."

He looked embarrassed. His head was low, and he scanned the long carpet under his feet. "It's fine. I know this must sound pretty silly."

It did. It wasn't the concept of witches she found hilarious. She was, after all, a young woman who could see dead people. She was attuned to the possibilities of supernatural forces and beings. What she laughed at was the idea of *those people* being witches. She immediately imagined Vincent, New York's most charming and popular entertainer, wearing a black pointed hat like the ones in children's books. And she saw Clarissa by his side, smoking a long cigarette and only pretending to be interested. Margarite had difficulty seeing her enthusiastic about anything outside of her musical number. "I apologize." She giggled once more. "You're serious, aren't you?"

He nodded. "We use magic to find enlightenment. We are of our own creation, not associated with the more infamous magic organizations you've probably read horror stories about."

"I can't say I'm familiar with any of it." She felt hot. The cape she'd been burdened with was stifling. She tried to play with Carrie's necklace through the fabric. That would calm her. The dull pain of nervousness stabbed at the bottom of her throat. *Witches? What could witches want with me?* Her mind immediately jumped to sacrifices and virgin blood for making bonds with the Devil. *No, that's only in stories.* Then she had a thought, one she was irritated it took her so long to realize. *They want my Sight.* She turned around and walked away.

"Wait!" Sal came running to her side.

"You just invited me up here to use me."

"No…" he said. He stumbled over several more words. "It's all in good fun."

"How did you know?"

Sal stared with a cloudy look in his eyes, obviously unsure how much to disclose.

"Is it so apparent? Do I speak to thin air? What, are you dead yourself? Is this a test?" She coughed a single sob, relieving the growing ache in her heart. Covering her face with her hands, she placed her long fingers under her eyes to catch dripping mascara.

Sal stood behind her for a moment. He nearly rested his hand on her shoulder, then retreated, clutching his lapel instead. "I hadn't a clue," he said. "Clarissa told me. She thought it'd be a good idea to invite you up."

"*She* told you?" Margarite swung her body around like a baseball bat. "Trying to embarrass me? How does she know?" Her eyes filled with rage.

Sal stepped back and stared at her.

"I asked you a question, Salvatore."

His lips quivered. He shook his head to focus his thoughts. "You gave her a fright. Said you were talking with Douglas at the theater."

"A fright? How could a simple old stagehand—" She stopped herself. Douglas. The red-haired man who wanders the stairs saying he's just looking things over. She took him for some kind of security guard. How did she miss the signs? "He's dead, isn't he?"

He nodded. "Heart attack. Few months before you joined the company. Real nice guy. He was close with Clarissa."

Margarite felt a horrible combination of sadness and stupidity wash over her. "Were they lovers?"

"No," Sal said, grinning. "Not at all. Douglas just took care of her. Not everyone at the theater was so kind to her and Bigs when they started. But Old Doug made sure those opinions were kept at bay." His eyes became sad. His voice creaked. "Sometimes even by force."

Margarite raised her eyebrow. "But why would anyone be cruel to Clarissa? Is she…"

"Oh!" Sal looked at his watch. "We'll be late. Let's go."

❖

The room was large and sparsely furnished, a round table in its center adorned with candles and several chairs. Nobody was sitting in them yet; all guests to *that* party were standing against the olive-colored walls. They held drinks and cheerfully carried on conversation as if it were perfectly normal to hug the perimeter of a large room. As Margarite entered, one very curvaceous woman took notice. She whispered something to her companion, a man of about forty. He then turned to someone else, and that someone else to someone else. Soon all eyes and conversations were focused on her and Sal.

"Gee," she said, "nice to see all of you, too." The room's occupants nervously giggled. Margarite took inventory of their faces. From *Weinstein's Wonderacts* she counted four chorus girls, one stagehand, and two musicians. She recognized Missy Charles from the revue on Forty-Second and Sing Sing Walker from the all-black show on Fiftieth. They hadn't been downstairs earlier, so they must have come especially for this gathering. Clarissa peeked out from behind Mr. Walker's shoulder. She timidly smiled.

Margarite immediately wanted to pull her aside and clear the air about Douglas. Had she known anything about the relationship between them, she would have brought him up more delicately. Hell, if she even knew the man wasn't a man at all, but a spirit haunting the theater, she would have approached the situation entirely differently. She started over to Clarissa. The room gasped. Sal grabbed her arm and pulled her into him.

"You can't go in there yet," he whispered.

The others looked a wreck, clutching their hearts and fanning themselves from fright. Some of them were pointing to the floor. Margarite looked down. She was tiptoeing dangerously close to a line made of salt that swooped around the room. One giant circle had been drawn with it on the circumference of the table.

"It's a protection circle," Sal added.

"From what?"

"Dark spirits during the séance."

She blanched. "We don't need to do a séance. I can see the souls as they are."

"But surely there are souls you can't see. We will summon them."

Margarite's muscles twitched, ready to move. She didn't want to invite more ghosts to her side. She already had access to plenty. She broke free from Sal's grip and turned for the door.

Harold Roth came barging in, waving a metal canister in the air. "I've got it. Had to ask cook—" He slammed right into her. The container flew from his hand and landed inside the circle with a sharp clang. The lid popped off and salt spilled everywhere.

"Damn, Harold," Clarissa exclaimed. "Now this will take forever to get right."

Harold sighed and looked at Margarite. He was holding her in his arms instinctively to keep her from falling over after the collision. "I apologize, Miss Duff."

Margarite blushed. A smile crept across her face. *Mr. Roth knows me?* She cleared her throat. "Please, Mr. Roth, call me Margarite."

"Yes. And you may call me Harold." Sal nudged him and raised his eyebrows. "Oh," Harold said. He let go of Margarite. Both men quickly looked in Clarissa's direction. Margarite did the same. She was busy discussing how to retrieve the salt with Sing Sing and Missy.

Sal seemed relieved. "I'll go find Vincent." He carefully slid against the wall behind the others.

Harold turned back to Margarite. "I really shouldn't have been running like that. Just excited to get started. Thank you for coming tonight. To the party. And to this. I know you must think it's unusual and all. And yes, it is."

"I'm thankful for the invitation. It's a lovely home."

"Yes. Yes. Big. But lovely. Can't say I take much credit for anything." He laughed awkwardly.

The room was disturbed again by Vincent's arrival. He burst in through another door that could easily have been mistaken for a closet. "Not to worry, not to worry!" He pointed to Clarissa. "This can be fixed." He gingerly stepped toward the circle. Then in it. Again, the guests were in a fright. "Gasp all you want, you old thingamabobs. Nothing has been consecrated yet." He kneeled down. "It's just salt!" He dipped his finger into the circle, then touched his tongue and scrunched up his face.

Everyone was nervously murmuring. Sal spoke up to ease the crowd. "Vincent, I'll get a broom."

"Darling," Vincent said, "let me take care of it." He kissed the air twice and turned his attention to the floor.

Sal's cheeks flushed.

Vincent walked around the circle to the pile of spilled salt, then he faced the crowd and smirked. He was suddenly onstage. He started singing. *"Look for the silver lining..."* He picked up the canister and drummed against it, moving around the space as a sliver of salt poured from its mouth. *"Whene'er a cloud appears in the blue."* It collected on the floor in an intricate pattern. *"Remember somewhere the sun is shining..."* He tapped the tip of his shoe at the spilled salt, moving it around like one would draw in the sand at the beach. *"And so the right thing to do is make it shine for you."*

When he was finished with his dance, Vincent struck a pose, creating the perfect button at the end of the number where applause should have begun. But his audience was more intrigued by the display at his feet. He had arranged the salt in a giant geometric pattern that filled the entirety of the circle. Symbols and stars and knots lay on the floor like one of the Persian rugs downstairs. "*Now*," he said, "the circle is consecrated." He pointed to a specific part of the circle near the windows. It had been broken with his heel. "Enter there. Find your seats. I'll close it once we are all settled." Margarite surveyed the room again. Everyone was rather young, mostly in their twenties, but maybe the oldest was forty. Definitely not what she expected from witches. In fairy stories, witches were old. Ugly. These practitioners were young and beautiful. And Vincent appeared to be the ringleader. Head witch. Whatever it was called. As a man no more than twenty-six, he certainly didn't seem old enough to be the master of any kind of magic. How did he gain that position?

Everyone began to file through the designated opening. Margarite fought against the current of bodies trying to get to Sal, who was at the far end of the room. "Pardon me... excuse me...I'm just...trying...to...reach..." Finally, she was close to him. She wriggled her hand between two women and grabbed his.

"Nervous?" he asked.

"You still haven't told me what I'm doing here."

"Just participate. I don't want to put anything in your head. No expectations."

Clarissa pulled herself forward by grabbing Sal's shoulder with her long fingers. "Margarite. Thank you for coming," she said. Her face was as still as stony as ever, and her voice didn't sound particularly gracious or welcoming or any of the other feelings that should accompany such a greeting.

Minutes prior, Margarite had felt bad for upsetting her, for bringing up Douglas when it wasn't clear that he was dead. But Clarissa's dryness, her vacant attempt at making Margarite feel welcomed in a strange place, erased those sympathetic feelings. Clarissa was still a bitch. "I hear I owe my invitation to you," said Margarite. "I should be thanking you." She smiled larger than she ever had before and gave her a big, ugly wink.

Clarissa made a humming-moan and raised her eyebrows. "Ain't she becoming a little bearcat." She leaned closer and whispered into her ear. "I told Harold this wasn't the place for newbies like you. But he insisted. I hope you're not easily spooked." She turned to Sal. "Sit by me, chickadee." She grabbed his hand and scooted past Margarite into the circle.

By the time Margarite navigated her way through the designated entrance, only one seat didn't appear to be obviously reserved. It was between two people she hardly knew: an understudy from the chorus and Missy Charles from the revue on Forty-Second. She was a big fan of Missy's. Actually, she served as a sort of inspiration for Margarite's stage persona. Missy was tall-ish, rail thin, and decidedly awkward. She had somehow harnessed her strangeness, molded it, and created a character that could be both laughed at *and* with. Weinstein recognized how successful this type was and had been searching for the perfect girl to recreate it in his show. Margarite possessed such qualities, and now her version of Missy Charles was giving the genuine article a run for her money. Missy communicated her annoyance by a specific glower aimed at Margarite when she sat down.

When everyone was settled, Vincent walked to the table with a woman on his arm. "Friends, I have the pleasure of introducing you to a very special lady. We're honored to have her with us. Georgiana." He stepped to the side and clapped. The room joined in.

Georgiana was a small woman, both in height and width, and about forty years old. Her hair was black and her skin bronze. An oversized brown lace shawl hung from her shoulders, just below a cascade of golden rings that dangled from her ears. She looked like many of the women from Margarite's neighborhood, definitely not from America. "Thank you, thank you," she said. Her accent, unidentifiable as it was, was thicker than Margarite had expected. It sounded more like *Zank you, zank you.*

Vincent pulled out a chair for her next to Clarissa. Georgiana glanced at her once and stepped back. She pointed to the other chair, the one reserved for Vincent next to Harold Roth. There was a misunderstanding about where she preferred to be, but eventually it was settled. Nobody in the room said anything, but she clearly didn't want to be too close to Clarissa.

Clarissa stared straight ahead, gripping a silver fan so hard it probably would never open again.

Finally they were ready to begin. Vincent explained it was the group's first time performing a séance, and they were thrilled to be initiated by Georgiana.

"Place the hands on the table," said Georgiana. "Both of them." She held her two hands up, then placed them flat on the surface of the table to instruct the group. They complied. "Now we need to close the eyes." *Cloz ze eyez.* In addition to the accent, she also seemed to have a speech impediment. People squinted their eyes and strained their ears to concentrate on what she was saying. She opened her eyes wide, then shut them to demonstrate. "Now I will call upon spirits. See if any are near who would like to join. Remain eyes closed until I say."

While Georgiana rattled a poetic, albeit butchered, call to the *other side*, Margarite silently laughed to herself. No ghosts were in that room. She'd have seen them. And even if there were spirits wandering around the house, which there probably weren't, why would they listen to Georgiana and stop in for a chat with a bunch of drunken strangers?

"The room is charged. The energy right for the souls to communicate. Keeping your eyes shut, you must now slide your hands over to your neighbor's." The sound of palms, some wet and some dry, sliding on the polished wood was strange. One person's were too damp and made a squeak. Several people laughed. Georgiana hushed them. "No matter what, you must not let go of the hands. Breaking the circle breaks the energy. Can I hear you all agree to this?"

Silence.

"I must hear you agree to the terms."

The participants collectively murmured a version of *yes.*

"Now you may open the eyes."

The room was surprisingly darker than before. The candles in the middle of the table burned a little less boldly, the orange flames reduced to merely their blue centers. A chill wriggled up Margarite's spine. It was suddenly cool in there. Something about the air was still. Not that it had been *moving* or anything like that before. It just felt placid. At ease. Margarite tried to articulate the room's atmosphere in her mind, but she couldn't find the words. It just had to be felt. And the feeling she had at that moment was unlike anything she'd had before. She'd seen ghosts her whole life, never requiring a drastic change of energy to do so. Communicating with the deceased came naturally to her. What kind of crazy stuff was this Georgiana pulling so that she could do the same?

Margarite snuck a peek in her direction. The medium's eyes were wide. She appeared frightened.

"The...the...souls. I am...trying to capture one with my mind." Her eyes darted around the table. "Does anyone have someone they would like to speak to? I can attempt to beckon them."

Without missing a beat, Clarissa spoke. "I do." Her lips were pursed, and she stared intensely.

Georgiana took a breath. "Who? Who would you like to speak to?"

"He knows who he is," she said. Then her head turned to the medium. "That should be enough."

Georgiana swallowed. "Sprits, I call upon you to bring this woman whom she asks. A...male..." She referred to Clarissa for confirmation. A nod. "A male. If this soul is present, please step forward." *Plez ztep fowad.*

She held the Circle captive with anticipation. Their faces froze waiting to see her register the presence of the ghost.

"If you cannot show yourself, give a sign. Let us know you are here."

A signal from a ghost seemed to make the room more nervous than the sight of one. Margarite observed the crowd looking at potential items that could create such a sign. The window behind Georgiana could come crashing in, the drapes surrounding it could unfurl violently across the table, the crystal chandelier could at best tinkle, or at worst, fall. Missy's hand was becoming increasingly clammy. Margarite wanted to shake it off, but she feared breaking the group's bond.

A floorboard creaked.

Georgiana's face blanched. Her pupils seemed to pulsate, and her forehead broke out in a sweat. She stammered. "Good...good evening...little one."

Clarissa spoke up. "That's not—"

Vincent hushed her. He was captivated by the display.

"Thank you," said Georgiana. "I am the only one to speak to the spirits." She scowled at Clarissa. "Open your mouth too much and one might just crawl in."

Clarissa sank into her seat. Her expression became dark.

"The male...the boy." She searched for words. When she found them, she barreled through. "Black skin and coarse hair. He misses his mother. He misses life. He cries."

That's when Margarite stopped listening. She peered around the room. There was no boy there. There was no spirit there at all. Her eyes met Clarissa's. They seemed to say, *you know this is a lie.*

The medium continued her reading. She went on and on about the afterlife, about the variety of souls around them— none of it true according to what Margarite observed. The caustic sound of that woman's voice eventually began to drown in other noises. The floor creaked again. The crystal chandelier did, indeed, tinkle. The flames on the candles morphed from small orbs to long funnels and back again. The Circle became uneasy. Someone shrieked. "Stay connected," Georgiana instructed. "I…will make it end."

Clarissa leaned back, still holding on to Sal and Harold. She investigated under the table behind her. Again, she looked at Margarite as if to communicate that she was searching for some trickery, maybe rigging on the floor to create such illusions. She shrugged.

The floor creaked once more, this time at a very specific spot in the far corner near the door. Margarite focused her attention there. She saw an oval mirror hung on the wall above a decorative table. She noticed the reflection was cloudy, as if it'd been smeared with wax. She tilted her chair back to get a better look. The smears moved, actually more like smoke than wax. She reclined farther, until she risked breaking her partners' grasps. Now she could see the whole mirror clearly.

A shadow emerged from the billows of smoke. A face, not her own or anyone else's in that room, stared back at her.

She screamed and fell from the chair.

The Circle was broken.

❖

Sal and Vincent were sitting with Margarite when she came to. "There she is," Vincent said. Her eyes were fluttering. "Rita took a fall, didn't she?"

She raised her head. It felt too heavy to do so. It plopped back down onto a cushion underneath. "Who?"

"Margarite is too formal and I think you have a goofy streak. Rita is more fitting."

She groaned and stretched. Her hands grazed satin. She was on a couch in a room with red and gold walls. "Where am I?"

"Recovery," Sal said. His tone was flat. He coughed a laugh afterward.

She heard a door open. "Oh, good! She's awake!" said Harold. He was carrying a tray with a glass of water.

"Darling," said another voice. It was Clarissa's unmistakable holler. "What are you carrying that for? That's why you hired maids." Margarite shifted her head more. Clarissa was frantically smoking and pacing on the far side of the room.

"I'm so embarrassed. Leave it to the new girl to make a fool of herself at the party. I'm sorry for ruining things."

"No matter," Clarissa said. "That lady is a load of shit."

Harold handed Margarite the glass and smiled. He went to Clarissa. The boys helped her sit up so she could drink. After a few gulps, the pain started to subside. She smacked her lips. A tangy aftertaste lingered on the sides of her tongue. "There's something in this."

"Some oils. Pain-relieving tonic," said Vincent.

Sal smirked. "Witches' brew."

"So," Vincent said, getting down to business, "what did you think?"

"I'm sorry. I don't understand what I'm—"

Vincent scoffed. "Come on, Rita. No need for niceties.

We know you can see the dead. This medium, she's new to us. Was she legitimate?"

Clarissa barreled over. In addition to a cigarette, she was now holding a glass of brown liquor. "Of course she wasn't legitimate. She was lying through those rotten teeth of hers. That boy she saw, if she saw one at all, wasn't mine. I told you I—"

Harold took her by the arm. "Clar, we believe you. We're just confirming—"

"With *her*," she said. Her attitude could sear skin. "She's the only one who can do anything right nowadays. You're all falling under her spell. She knows how to do the number better than me, she knows the truth even though I already told it to you." She turned to Harold. "What? Is she going to *know* you more than me soon, too?"

Harold pulled her in closer. "Angel, please calm down."

Clarissa yanked her arm back. Her drink fell to the floor. "Shit," she said. Then she stormed out.

Sal and Harold both spoke at the same time, "I should—" They claimed Clarissa in different ways, Harold as a lover and Sal as a best friend. Margarite smiled at the thought. What must that be like?

Vincent tapped Margarite's leg. "Up, up." She squirmed upright so he could sit on the couch with her. "Let's chat."

"There was no boy," said Margarite. "She completely made it up. Ghosts are either here or they're not. They can't be summoned."

Vincent frowned. "What a waste."

"But maybe other things can be."

His interest was piqued. "Go on."

"I've never seen anything like it before, but she did manage to call upon something. Or maybe it wasn't even her. Maybe it was all of us together. Whatever it was that happened, the sounds and the movements in the room were real. And she was surprised. I think she panicked and made the boy up. Clarissa was an easy target."

He didn't acknowledge the medium's deception. "What did *you* see up there?"

She struggled with whether or not she should be honest. It was already crazy enough to admit to seeing dead people. Describing what she saw in that mirror was crazier. Then she reminded herself that they all claimed to be witches. The rules of sanity were clearly not at play here. "A face. It wasn't in the room. Or maybe it was. I could only see it in the mirror."

He was close and intense. "What did it look like?"

"Dark. Deep purple or indigo or black. I can't describe it. It was..."

"What? It was what?"

"It wasn't like anyone, no, any*thing* I've ever seen before."

Vincent leaned his head back and grinned. "It's working." He laughed. "It's working!"

"What's working?" she asked. He didn't answer. He kept smiling and giggling to himself. Margarite's tolerance for everyone's vagueness was wearing thin. "I'm going to need you all to stop being so spooky about this Circle. I haven't been a part of one before. I don't know the rules or what you've done in the past or what your goals are."

His laughter turned maniacal. "Rita! You are a godsend!" He hugged her, jolting her head a little too quickly for comfort. She grimaced. "For months I've been trying to bring forth beings from the other side. Finally! His rituals are working!"

"Who? Whose rituals? Sal?"

"No," he said. His expression warmed. "Hasis. He is my teacher and friend. You must meet him."

❖

Margarite hated to be among the first to leave, but she was finished. The several drinks she had after her fall probably weren't the best idea, but the boys insisted they'd make her headache go away, at least until morning. She tried not to appear drunk as she weaved through the now-groggy party. Its heartbeat had slowed, guests finding chairs, walls, or that night's lover to lean against. The laughter had turned to giggles, the dancing to staggering, and the trumpet to a piano. She walked out a side door with hopes she could slip away unnoticed. The breeze coming off the water was cooler than she expected, the first sign of summer's looming departure. Autumn was somewhere in that wind, tapping on her shoulders and making her wish she'd not left Vincent's cape upstairs.

She made her way across the pebbles of the footpath to the cars. The moon cast the house's mammoth shadow across the grounds. A cloud of smoke rolled into the air from someone smoking ahead. "I see she's escaping," Clarissa said.

Margarite jumped. "You startled me."

"Couldn't see the Negro in the night, could you?" Clarissa stepped into the light from a window. Her face was tired and sad.

"No, that's not what startled me. Anybody would give a person a fright hiding on the side of the house like this." Clarissa rolled her eyes and exhaled. "Why must you do that? Why do you assume I'm a vicious woman that hates you?"

"Because most people are terrible, honey." Her typical confidence was gone. "You don't know what it's like to be me."

"You're right. But please stop acting like nobody else has ever had a tough time. I'm an orphaned immigrant girl who can see dead things. Life hasn't been easy for me, either."

Clarissa shrugged.

"And you know what? If weren't for everyone in this

show trying to hide the fact, I wouldn't have even known you were different."

"Because I'm not different," Clarissa said. "I'm a person putting on a show. Just like you."

"Even more reason to cut the bitch act. It's tiresome." She dashed around her toward the driveway. As she approached the corner, Margarite felt her face get warm, something that always happened when she got riled up about an issue.

"Hey, chickadee," Clarissa called. "I apologize. I'm no good at meeting new people. And tonight, especially, I'm a little thrown."

"There wasn't a boy up there," Margarite squeaked as her face cooled. "I'm sure you know that. I told everyone." Finally she turned to her. "Why didn't you say something? Why'd you let her put on such a show?"

Clarissa laughed. "I'm Clarissa Jenkins, a strong, talented, and elegant woman. I'm a force to be reckoned with. But if I went off on that lady at the table, it'd be strictly emotional. I'd be mad as hell. And I'd be hurt. People don't need to see that version of me."

"But doesn't the Circle know about you?"

"Yes. But advanced as they are, some of them are still working through opinions and prejudices. So I do my best to keep from reminding them." Her voice caught in her throat, she cleared it. "Why you heading out so soon?"

Margarite shook her head and played with Carrie's necklace. "Tired, I guess. Want to save my energy for the show."

"Good of you. Hey, I don't want to make it seem we invited you upstairs just to use you. I mean, that is exactly what we did, but I don't like it. You're a good person, Margarite." She held out her hand. "I'd like to be friends."

Earlier in the night, Margarite wouldn't have trusted that truce offer, but the woman who stood in front of her now was different. She imagined this side of Clarissa was the one Sal was so fond of. "Please," Margarite said, "call me Rita."

Something happened. In that very moment. She shifted inside, like her internal organs had finally found the correct place to rest. The world suddenly felt *different*. Her body was lighter, her senses more attuned. It was wonderful and scary and mysterious, and the chance to take Clarissa's hand at that moment was part of it. So she did.

VINCENT

Summer 1922

"She's having a breather outside," Harold said. He kneeled on the ground to pick up Clarissa's spilled drink.

"Honestly, Roth, call someone up to take care of that," said Vincent. "Clarissa often just talks out her ass, but she's right about this. If you're paying for the help, use them."

"It's all a song and dance, you know that. I'm perfectly capable of doing this by myself. They're just here to keep this place in order." He groaned and stood, cupping the broken glass in his hand. "They work for this house more than they work for me." He walked to a bin and carefully placed the shards in it. "Anyway, where's Sal?"

"I sent him downstairs with Rita. A few cocktails will make her feel better." Vincent walked over to the butler's table near the door and poured two drinks. He handed one to Harold. "I thought we should be alone for a moment. Debrief."

"Yes, yes." Harold swallowed a sip of brandy. "You think this kid's the real deal?"

"Positively." Vincent became embarrassed. "I'm incredibly jealous of her." It was unlike him to speak of vulnerability, but he'd been consciously trying to do it. Vulnerability was the opposite of strength. Embracing the poles of life was important for someone with ambitions like his. The Complete Man needed to master all emotions in order to control them. After he made his confession of jealousy, he felt as if a small moth had flown away from the light inside him. He shined just a tad brighter without it there. He sighed in relief.

"What will you do? Try and learn her talents? I don't think even she understands what she's doing, not enough to teach you."

"I can't learn from her, Roth." Vincent showed his temper by emphasizing the *th*. He caught himself. "She's a natural witch. There are many things I can learn, but not what she's capable of. Yet. I need to further my studies. There are ways to advance to her level. Maybe even beyond." He was getting tongue-tied. He inhaled, tried to focus, and continued delicately. "You know I've spent months trying to summon these beings."

"Christ, not this again." Harold slammed his drink back.

"These beings have so much to teach me."

"We've done the blessings, the money spells, and the protection spells. We don't need to go asking ghosts and ghoulies for advice. What we're doing is working."

"I've had a thought recently. What if all the rituals we've performed are just rituals. No magic, just poetry and performance." Harold waved a dismissive hand, but Vince continued. "Maybe you've kept your fortune because you're doing it right, maybe the show is a hit because we're really talented and the work is good. We're just positively reinforcing all the great stuff we already do."

"Then let's just keep doing that. Because it's working."

He held Harold's shoulders. "Her being here tonight was the first time I really *felt* something. I felt magic." He realized how intense he was being, that his passion was probably too strong for his friend. He backed off. "I've relentlessly tried to summon forces from the other side and I haven't seen any results. I've fasted and prayed and studied for nothing. I thought about giving up. But she saw something in that room. She saw what I've been trying to. My attempts are not in vain. I just can't communicate with them yet. She can help me and I can learn. Really learn."

❖

Vincent waited nervously at the bottom of the stairs of the 207th Street station. He didn't care for immigrant neighborhoods. Hell's Kitchen, just blocks from Broadway, was bad enough. This area, Inwood, was newer and attracted a more assorted crowd. All the folks who couldn't fit in tenements downtown were moved up there. Or they were workers. Real burly, rough types hired to do labor on some new development. He didn't know exactly what. Anyway, people like that frightened him. In Midtown, he marched down streets with confidence, but he walked with tight limbs in that northern neighborhood, like a closed-up flower shielding itself from harsh night air.

After the rumbling of the train ceased, he saw Rita on the stair. She was dressed plainly, just like him. *Good*, he thought. *Don't want to attract attention up here.*

"Thank goodness you've arrived," he said, throwing his arms around her and kissing her on both cheeks.

She looked around for a clock. "Am I late?"

"No, no. I'm just chronically early. And I get jumpy in these derelict neighborhoods." A man walked by wearing a muddy jumpsuit and carrying a steel lunch box. "And why is everyone covered in filth? I feel as if I'm in a coal mine."

Rita stared at him oddly. "You don't keep up with the papers, do you Vincent?"

"Maybe for the reviews, dear." He laughed.

"Of course everything is dirty. They're building tunnels." He cocked his head.

"For the new train system. The clouds of dirt drift clear across the island."

"Oh. Well, you learn something new every day." He stepped into the street to get his bearings. He pointed west. "We need to go this way." She took the arm he offered her. "Was your ride enjoyable? Where are you coming from, again?"

"It was fine, thank you. I come from Hell's Kitchen. A little...what did you say? That's right, a *derelict* neighborhood near the theater." She smiled slyly.

Vincent's bout of embarrassment didn't last long, as Rita was a good sport. She explained that she was perfectly aware of how seedy certain areas of the city could be, particularly where she lived. But those were the cards she'd been dealt, and she was accustomed to it. "And besides," she said, "it's not all bad there. Most people are just trying their best." Vincent attempted to understand. After all, Salvatore was the son of Italian immigrants and he loved him dearly. He secretly vowed to himself to be less judgmental. What was the opposite of being judgmental? Accepting? He made a mental note to think on that, and learn to master both.

They ventured down 207th until they hit the woods. Trees towered overhead, sloping up and down the rocky terrain. This part of Manhattan was, until recently, only accessible by car. Its natural state made it the perfect place for the rich to build country residences. Several roofs peeked above the canopy in the distance to prove it. Most of them were no longer in use, though. The development of the area made it less appealing. Public transportation allowed just about anyone to tromp on their slice of heaven. So the wealthy moved to more fashionable places, leaving the forest to claim what it could.

As delicate as he led others to believe he was, Vincent was not fearful of the forest. He was raised just north of the city, in Dutchess County. His childhood home was already very old when he was born, situated on a hillside near an ancient waterfall. It was a picturesque and magical place radiating with histories and memories. He spent many summer days exploring forests and caves, searching for faerie circles or elfin homes in old oak trees. His parents were Spiritualists and encouraged such ideas.

These beliefs were popular then. It wasn't uncommon for him to overhear discussions regarding the occult or to spy on séances held in the dining room after he was put to bed. His lullabies were prayers to ancestors; his favorite songs were chants to nature goddesses. When he was old enough, he studied their literature and learned how to be an active member in their ceremonies. After he discovered his love of theater, his time was split between rehearsing and performing rituals to ensure his success. He was so indoctrinated with magical ideas, he had a difficult time deciphering the difference between true talent and the gifts bestowed to him through asking the spirits. For sanity's sake, he liked to believe it was a combination of both. So nature and all it had to offer was, in a way, Vincent's home.

"I come here often," he said. "I'm very familiar with this forest. Don't worry."

The footpaths from the street only took them so far. Soon they diverged from what appeared to be a well-trodden route and were walking in deer trails. "I'm glad I wore slacks," Rita said. "I'd have lost a dress twenty minutes ago going down that hill." She peered around. "It's nice to be away from buildings and street traffic. No wonder you enjoy it here."

He nodded. "I like to imagine this is what New York was like long ago, back when the first explorers came. Nothing but trees and Indians."

Summer had made the forest floor thick with flora that veiled the rocky ground below. Just as Vincent would find his footing on a boulder, he'd have to crawl back down to loosen Rita's boot from a hidden crevice. Eventually they rose several feet above the brush, onto a series of large rocks that were haphazardly piled on top of one another up a hillside. They were long and smooth, as if at the beginning of time a titan had used them like a human would sprinkle rice so as not to get lost in confusing terrain. They'd fallen in piles, creating hundreds of caves in the empty spaces between them. "Natives used these," he said. He peeked his head into one. "You can still see soot from their fires. Pottery and such, too. Now only *he* lives here."

"Hasis," Rita said, stepping up to his level. She kneeled to look inside. "He lives in a cave like this?"

"Did you expect him to reside in the old Astor mansion?" He laughed and waved her forward to a particular rock formation around the next bend. It was removed from the other caves, with a cliff overlooking the Hudson River. "That's it."

Vincent had been there countless times, but he never stopped being surprised by its modesty. Every time he walked that path, he wondered how a person could live so minimally. Hasis knew more than anyone, had access to such great power. Why would he seclude himself all the way out here? He'd heard of men becoming hermits, stripping their lives of all luxury in order to find enlightenment. He figured Hasis was doing just that. Vincent, on the other hand, had no interest in such simplicity. He thought himself perfectly capable of advancing his knowledge while enjoying a nice cup of tea, preferably laced with whiskey. Every visit to Hasis's home was a test in endurance. What new tonic of bark and beetles would he be made to drink? Which waterfowl would be hacked up in front of him for divination? How many hides would be drying by the fire to make winter robes?

Today, there were a deer and some kind of large rodent. Nearby, three rudimentary cages were filled with birds, flapping and bouncing erratically as if their perches were made of hot coal instead of old branches. For a moment, Vincent felt embarrassed for bringing someone, especially a lady, to such a strange place. He glanced to Rita and was surprised by her expression. She appeared curious.

"I am not home," said a strangely accented voice from behind. They turned. Hasis stood there, in all his almost seven-foot glory. He wore the same long, black cloak that Vincent had become so familiar with. It had once been decorated with intricate embroidery, but living in the elements had dulled its vibrancy. It now looked no different than a ratty theater curtain. His lithe, pallid arms protruded from it, like he was a scarecrow made of old birch branches. He carried a basket of cuttings in one hand, the other held regally above his heart. "Luckily I found provisions during my morning stroll. Now we will have plenty of time to converse." He acknowledged Rita. "You must be the witch. I am Atrahasis. It is a name you might have known, were you properly trained, like in the old days."

She spoke with a nervous tremor. "It's v-very good to meet you." She was caught in the gaze of his large, blue eyes. They lent the only color to his face, which was void of all blush in the cheeks and lips. His hair was so light it was indistinguishable from the skin on his forehead. Vincent recalled feeling similar wonder when he first laid eyes on him two years earlier. The memory brought both a slight smile to his face and a shiver down his spine.

Hasis walked them to his home. Like the table at the séance, a ring of salt also surrounded his cave. This was a coarser grain than the cooking kind used at the mansion, and herbs had been crushed into the mixture. When Hasis approached it, he waved his hand near the ground. The salt blew away and created an opening for them to walk through.

Rita gasped.

"Do not be too impressed by my…what do you call them, Vincent? My *parlor tricks*." He smiled a wide crocodile smile and gestured for them to take a seat in front of the cave's opening. He closed the circle with another wave of his hand. A small boulder and two milk crates were set out around a tiny fire that barely crackled. It must have been lit the night prior, left to burn out by itself. Hasis excused himself as he brought his basket through a curtain at the entrance of the cave.

While they waited for him to return, Vincent tried to smile at Rita, but she was too consumed studying her surroundings.

Hasis reappeared with an iron pot he placed over the minuscule flame. He threw a handful of the flowers he'd harvested inside, immediately producing a smell both sweet and bitter. He took a seat on the rock and folded his hands in his lap. "Do begin," he said.

Rita looked to Vincent for help. He spoke up. "As I explained, Rita has seen what I cannot. It is my intention to help her recognize her skills so that we may work together."

Hasis leered at her. "You have no Mistress? An elder witch to teach you the Way?"

"No," she replied. "I was not raised with these beliefs. Or any, for that matter."

"That is why beliefs die. They are ignored." He shifted on his rock. "Some call it the *Way of Things*. The some who follow it, at least. They are few, especially here in this country." He was quiet for a moment. He closed his eyes and breathed through his tiny nostrils. "I can teach you, like I have taught Vincent and many others. But you will be different. You have real powers. A natural witch, not a learned one."

Vincent felt that pang of jealousy toward her again. He knew Hasis was referring to him. *A learned one.*

Hasis continued, focused solely on Rita. "To ignore the gifts given to you by the Way is to be responsible for balance being broken. When balance is uneven, chaos ensues. You do not want that, do you?"

She writhed in her seat, stretched her neck, and exhaled. "Tell me, what is expected of a natural witch?"

Hasis's eyes widened with pleasure. "Witches are mortals. They live and die, like all the others. Some can live longer if they have mastered certain manipulations of nature. From there, the roles and powers of your kind are varied. A witch is typically born with one gift. We call this your Paramount." He paused, presumably a technique to ensure she retained information. "Your Paramount is Sight. Beyond that, your powers must be studied, just like my current student here."

Again, Vincent felt rage flash through his body. He believed magic was magic, no matter how it was attained. Some were natural witches and some, actually most, were learned. Being in the presence of someone like Rita made him realize how much harder he needed to work to achieve his goal. The gift she was born with would take him years, even a whole lifetime to understand. And that was just communication with the spirit realm. The laundry list of powers he needed to master to become a Complete Man began to give him heart palpitations.

Hasis stood and went to one of the cages. He opened the door and snaked his hand around a small brown bird. It chirped and bounced, panicked by the sudden attention. Hasis corralled it into a corner, opened his palm, and closed his eyes.

When he opened them seconds later, the bird was calm. It froze on its branch, only its chest moving from nervous breaths. He carefully grabbed it and removed it from the enclosure.

"Witches with your Paramount are integral to the balance of the Way," he said, stroking the tiny bird's head. "You are part of the journey for the deceased to find peace. You currently just observe these souls, but you are meant to assist them. You and your kind are the only beings that can always see and speak to spirits." In one swift gesture, Hasis squeezed the bird's head, twisted it, and threw it into the boiling pot. He held its body out on his long, flat hand. "You see?"

Vincent fell backward off his stool. "Geez, man," he said. "You trying to scare her half to death?"

Hasis whipped his head in his direction, eyes blazing.

"Wait," Rita said, saving him from a scolding. "I see." Her voice quaked. "I see its soul."

Hasis refocused his attention on her. "Good, my girl. Now let it see you."

Vincent wanted to stand and brush himself off, but he was stuck to the ground in awe. He watched Rita move close to Hasis's hand, the carcass still bleeding in it. She cocked her head, and she spoke. "It's all right, little one. Come here." She held up her finger. "Right here." She waited and gasped. "It's on my hand," she whispered. Her eyes were fixed there. "Can you see it?" Vincent shook his head. "Of course not. How silly of me." After about a minute, she flicked her wrist and watched the sky.

"Very good," said Hasis.

"I've never seen anything die before." She faced him, her face red hot. Angry tears coursed down her cheeks. She gritted her teeth. "Don't you ever do that in front of me again." Her eyes flashed from blue to green, then back again.

Vincent felt sick. The two people he needed most were

at odds. He tried to figure out something to say to put Rita at ease.

Hasis beat him to it. "Oh, child," he said. "You must develop a thicker skin than that. Especially if you are to embrace your gifts, which I hope you will. Vincent needs all the help he can get."

Rita wiped her hands on her pants, as if a real bird had just been perched her finger. "I'm still unclear about what I can do to help him."

Hasis turned to Vincent with a very specific glare, one that almost seemed to get right inside his head and ask, *You haven't told her yet?*

As Vincent shook off his teacher's stare, Hasis answered her question. "Vincent has ambition. More than any man I have seen a while. And I have been around for a very long while." He reached for the bottom of his robe and wiped the blood from his hands. "Ambition is not something to frown upon. People with ambition do things. People with ambition change the world. And the world needs changing, you know that? A war has ended and brought with it greed. Licentiousness. Poverty. Entire peoples being taken advantage of." His face lit up as if he had a new thought. "You are not from here, yes?"

She appeared very small. Her saucer eyes seemed to have shrunk to the button eyes of a child. "Scottish. I came here as a little girl."

"Something we have in common. It is not easy being a foreigner." Hasis waved at his humble cave and sighed. "And you are a lucky one. You are successful, not toiling the days away in a field or a tunnel or in a factory that is destined to roast you alive."

Rita bit her lip. Vincent knew her aunt was a seamstress. He wondered if the fire downtown had been a raw spot in their household.

"So now is the time to reach for power," continued Hasis, "now is the time for a Complete Man. Your Paramount will help my boy attain the assistance he needs from the other side. It will help him heal us."

Rita was quiet. She raised an eyebrow. "Why don't you teach him?"

He hummed. "My kind was born with special abilities that make most magic unnecessary. So while I have vast knowledge, I do not practice. One who does not practice cannot teach." He extended one hand to Vincent and the other, still stained with blood, to Rita. "Will you help him?"

Vincent knew that was his cue. He reached out, took Hasis's long hand, and looked to Rita. He grinned, hoping his enthusiasm would transfer to her.

She didn't return the smile. But she didn't frown either. She just took his hand. Firmly. She stared into Hasis's eyes with determination that both frightened and excited Vincent.

❖

Manhattan had too many distractions for magic, so most of the Circle's ceremonies were held out at Roth's mansion. It was quiet there, closer to nature. Plus, there was luxury. After a meeting, they could drink Harold's fine wines and enjoy a meal prepared by his chef. But the millionaire often went out of town. Lots of business to attend to.

Luckily, Harold had been in a pleasant mood before he departed and offered his home to Vincent to hold a gathering without him. "I've given the staff time off while I'm away," he said. "No reason to have them there without me. But the groundskeeper is a permanent resident. He'll let you in. Just be careful with the place. It isn't even close to being paid off."

What Harold didn't know was Vincent wasn't holding a

meeting for the whole Circle, but for just Rita and himself. Hasis had given them specific instructions about how to lay the scene for the ritual. These limited the acceptable locales in Manhattan, even on the island's most primordial parts, like the forests uptown. The incantations had to be recited at a spot with water to the north and a forest to the south. Roth's estate was perfectly situated in such a place. But most importantly, they had to perform the ceremony at ground level, as close to the earth as possible. Under it would be even better. Vincent certainly didn't have access to a basement. He lived on the sixth floor, for Christ's sake. The only other cellar he knew of was at the theater, but he wasn't about to perform rituals there. Too risky. So Roth's mansion it was.

Arriving at the seemingly abandoned estate was eerie. Vincent was accustomed to it being lit up like a marquee, but tonight it was dark. The only light came from two lampposts at the front door. They were gaslights, a nod to the home's history. Vincent found it silly to use such archaic technology when electricity was available. And especially on that night, the two flames cast a more stylized light than bulbs would. He felt like they were ancient Druids, standing amongst fire and stone with the sea before them. It was a little too immersive.

Vincent tried the door. Locked. "That batty old man is supposed to be here to let us in," he said, his head buzzing around looking for assistance.

Rita laughed. "Is he really batty or are you just frustrated you can't open the door?"

He stared at her and rolled his eyes, even though he was trying to kick that patronizing habit. It wasn't thoughtful. A man with his kind of ambition needed to appear more graceful. Halfway through the gesture, he caught himself and stopped. His gaze was stuck on a piece of paper lodged in the door frame. He snatched it, read it, and made a gruesome face.

"What's it say?" Rita asked.

"Dinner with my wife." He held it up to her. "And a drawing of an arrow pointing left."

Obviously the only thing to do was to walk left. There was no other doorway on the front of the house, just grand windows and bushes. But when they peeked around the left corner of the mansion, they saw a lantern glowing on the patio. Many patios, verandas, terraces, and alcoves were attached to the house, but this one was unique. It was laid with slate of many sizes, the kind that made Vincent momentarily homesick. Because his childhood home was situated in the mountains, many buildings utilized similar stone, all shades of blues and violet. The darkness of the floor was a beautiful contrast to the pastel green of the patina on copper window frames that made up the glass conservatory, Palm Court.

Harold liked to place the band in there during parties. The multiple windows gave the illusion of an outdoor performance, and the leaded glass roof allowed guests to stargaze. The tiles on the floor had been imported from Spain, the fountain at its center from a now-ruined monastery in Italy. When not used as a stage, the room was home to hundreds of rare plants, most of them secured on Harold's travels. Five antique Chinese birdcages filled with feathers of every color hung from the ceiling. To stand in that room was like standing in a rainforest.

That night, with only the moon and a single lantern to light the way, the Court appeared less appealing. The tropical leaves cast strange shadows on the ground, and the eyes of what seemed like one hundred birds glowed yellow, green, and gold. The oasis had been transformed into a haunted wood of fairy stories. "I don't feel comfortable with this," said Rita.

Vincent adjusted a bag hung from his shoulder so he could get leverage on the rusty door handle. It grated against the frame and opened with a thud. Birds squawked like he was a serpent attacking their nest. "Look, he's gone through all the trouble of keeping this open. We need to go in."

They were quick to get through the greenroom. It was too creepy for Rita's taste. "Let's just find a goddamned light switch and turn on anything that will glow." She found the doorway to the foyer and stroked the walls in search of a switch or a knob that would give them light. Once located, the chandelier came on with what sounded like a kick drum.

Vincent stood at the base of the stairs, looking up. "Quiet in here without a party, isn't it?"

"Too quiet," she said. She pulled her shawl tight around her arms. "I don't know how the man lives here. Let's do this and get it over with. And remember, you promised me dinner."

"I did."

"Well, now I'm requesting dessert, too."

He grinned. Rita was growing on him. She'd started as just another girl in the show. Then she was an experiment. Now she was becoming a friend. She wasn't as particularly warm with him as she appeared to be with Sal or Frankie, but they got along. He didn't know exactly why she agreed to work with him. Possibly the meeting with Hasis intrigued her. More likely, it frightened her. Whatever the reason, he was glad. She was developing a certain toughness that he enjoyed.

The door to the basement was seamlessly blended into the walnut wall at the bottom of the grand staircase, its brass knob inside a hidden compartment. Vincent opened the passageway as effortlessly as any normal door.

"Did Harold show you that?" she asked. "Does he know we're using the basement?"

He shook his head.

"Then how did you know to do that?"

"Roth and I are great friends. I'm around often. But he

likes to disappear down here every once in a while to do work. You'll see."

Another switch made a clunking sound that soon illuminated the stairway. It only took several steps down to understand why Harold Roth would need to go into a basement to work. Half the room was dedicated to storage—booze storage.

Rita gasped. "He's a bootlegger?"

"Darling, did you think he was anything else? How do you think people make money nowadays? This Prohibition was the best thing to ever happen to some of us."

Rita ran down the stairs and spun around to behold the overwhelming presence of so many bottles and barrels. "No wonder his parties are so lush."

"He'll get out of it soon. Start investing in railroad or something legitimate." Vincent took out a compass and waited for it to adjust. He gestured to the other side of the cellar. "This way."

Luckily, the area he'd decided on didn't require too much clearing out. That corner wasn't used for storage, as the tiny window at ground level was worn from years of leaking. It had rained a day prior, and the concrete was still damp. A bucket and a mop were permanent residents. Vincent used them to dry the space while Rita searched for supplies in the giant bag he'd been carrying.

Some of its contents were from his home: several candles, a canister of salt, two black robes, and a tin box filled with broken pieces of chalk. The more unusual items had been borrowed from Hasis: four small vials of oil and one large bottle for mixing them, a chart detailing how to draw the intricate circle required for that particular ritual, thirteen stone tablets with carvings of Roman numerals, a rudimentary dagger, and a carefully wrapped bowl made of black glass.

Rita placed them neatly on a wooden bench, just like the prop tables in the wings of the theater.

She lit the incense to begin cleansing the air. Meanwhile, Vincent chalked out the many symbols on the diagram. There were circles and pentagrams and lines and script in a forgotten language. "Do you know what this says?" asked Rita. She looked at the floor sideways, as if changing the angle would somehow make the words more legible.

"Some of them," said Vincent. He rose from his knees and dusted off his hands, arranging candles in very specific points of the drawing.

"Maybe it'd be good to know all of them." She waved smoke away from her face to investigate further. "What if these words have significance?"

"They do have significance. That's why I've been very careful about writing them correctly." He sprinkled salt in a circle around the ceremonial space. "Hasis worked diligently on creating this map. He said it's important for my version to be an exact copy. One incorrect line could throw the whole ritual in a different direction."

"Like turn one of us into a rabbit? There's a top hat upstairs. We can go on tour across the county."

He raised an eyebrow, then pointed to the stack of stone tablets. "Place those around the pentagram on the left, counterclockwise."

"What do these do?"

"Magic Squares. They're kind of like coordinates. It's where we're looking to reach."

Their last task was to lay the bowl in the center and fill it with wine, which was convenient given their surroundings. "The bowl is dark, the wine is dark. Like a black mirror," he said. "Let's put on these robes and get to it." He started to unbutton his shirt.

She placed the last Square on the floor. "What are you doing? Can't we just put the robe on over this?" She smoothed her simple slip dress.

He laughed. "These have been used in many rituals. They're sacred. What we're wearing isn't."

She grimaced and coughed. "Isn't that why we're burning all this stuff? Or using all that perfume over there?"

"No. That's for your body. That's not sacred either. Yet." He ripped off his shirt. Rita averted her eyes. "We'll stand back to back if it makes you more comfortable." He turned around. "Besides, you're pretty and all, but I'm not interested."

"Oh right. I forgot you're engaged." She laughed. Even in her nervous state, she was still able to crack a joke. He felt the energy of the room soften.

He was a man of the theater. He'd been undressed in front of nearly everyone, so showing skin wasn't something he felt shy about. His socks were the last to go. When his bare feet touched the cold floor, the hairs on his legs stood up. "Okay, ready?"

"Just a sec." He heard her struggle to unfasten something. She kicked her shoe across the room as she wrestled with her hose. Finally she said, "I'm ready."

Her voice sounded small to him. Vulnerable. Vincent became embarrassed. "I apologize for the strangeness of this night. We just need to do it correctly or else it won't work." The gravity of this moment suddenly hit him. His throat tightened. "I've dedicated too much time to this for it to fail."

"What do you mean?"

"I…" He had trouble coming up with the words. It was all so absurd to say. "I've had a rigorous preparation period. Daily prayers and study, periods of fasting, withholding pleasures, indulging in pleasures. To become the Complete Man, one must master all things. I've attempted to do all a human can. But now I'm at a point where I must turn to other realms for guidance."

"I know. You'll summon them, and I'll speak to them and tell you their instructions. I got the lecture from Hasis."

"Correct." He walked to the bench, poured the four small vials of oil into the large bottle, and swirled the contents around. He covered the top with his hands, and he quietly said a prayer. "Pour this in your palm and anoint yourself. Circles on your forehead, heart, and below your navel. Then quickly put on the robe." Vincent hurriedly followed his own instructions, and then placed the bottle on the ground behind him without looking at her. "Your turn. It's there next to you."

As he placed the robe over his head, he heard Rita squeal. "Holy cow! This burns!"

"It's the cinnamon oil. It will subside shortly." He turned around just as Rita slipped on her robe. She had an uncomfortable expression plastered onto her face.

"You have a red mark on your head," she said.

"So do you. Devil's kiss." He smiled.

She gasped.

"I'm kidding. Well, some people call it that, but it's not the Devil. Obviously. Just oil. Shall we?"

They kneeled on either side of the bowl. Vincent was casting, so he faced north toward the water. Rita faced the forest at the south. Candles were placed at east and west. "Their light helps create the reflection." Rita leaned over the bowl to see herself. "No, not like that. Stay upright." He adjusted her back and her head. "Stay facing me. Just peer down with your eyes. Get it?"

"I can just barely see up my nose."

"You'll see more once we do the evocation." He cleared

his throat. "Never fully face a being from other worlds. Just glance at them. Direct contact can seem threatening or, in some cases, serve as an invitation. It all depends on what responds to our call."

Rita swallowed and smacked her lips. They sounded dry. "You don't make this seem very fun, Vincent."

He put his hand on her shoulder. "Don't be afraid. Long ago, we had a strong relationship with the other side. Those days are forgotten. But we're bringing them back. It's like coming home." He tried to radiate courage, hoping she would absorb some of it. But he had fears, too. If the spirit realm was as vast as he was led to believe, how could he be sure the right entity would respond? What if something malevolent showed up instead? Or a trickster spirit that aimed to turn his world upside down? He tried to push those thoughts from his head.

Hasis had given him careful instructions. The ritual would work.

Vincent placed the script on the floor, put his hands in the air, and began to read. He called upon powers of the elements, asked for blessings from spirits of the sea and of the wood, called for protection from forgotten ancestors. Hasis had translated the chants into English but left the hymns in their native Sumerian dialect. "These melodies were made for these words," he had once said. "They cannot be altered. What you call upon is ancient. Show respect by singing in its tongue." So Vincent did. He'd spent days practicing proper pronunciation, even if he didn't completely understand the meaning of every word. His study of Sumerian wasn't rigorous, probably because there wasn't much to know about it. Most of the history of that age was lost.

After what seemed like an hour, the incantations were through. Vincent looked to Rita and said, "There's just one thing left to do." He picked up the dagger. It had a stone handle that had probably once been polished to a brilliant shine. The blade was a dull, unidentifiable metal. The engravings were nearly rubbed away. This piece was very important to Hasis, and it was with great pain that he lent it to Vincent. He'd sworn to take care of it and return it as soon as he could. He raised the dagger between their faces. "Don't worry. It won't be gruesome."

She nodded. Her breathing was shaky.

Vincent took the blade and slit the palm of his left hand. He made a fist over the bowl and squeezed what blood he could from the wound. As soon as the last drop splashed into the wine, the candles' flames rose and then dimmed. Just like the night of the séance. The tiny window let in a meager amount of light; the rest came from the small blue flames around them.

"Start scrying," he said.

"What?"

"Read the reflections. Just like I told you."

Rita put her head down and looked into the bowl.

"Not like that, remember?"

She apologized and raised her head, letting only her gaze fall to the wine's glossy surface. "I don't see anything."

"Keep staring. Relax. Breathe with me." Vincent too looked down at the bowl. He inhaled deeply and loudly, then he exhaled through his mouth in a slight whistle. "Just focus on your breath. Once you're relaxed, the visions will come to you." Vincent knew from experience. He'd made attempts at scrying before, but only got as far as the *cloud stage*. That was what other believers called the time when the veils between worlds lifted. A slight fog fills the mirror, sometimes accompanied by a swirling of color. According to Hasis, that's when the entities become present, but they are not visible to everyone. With Rita there, he hoped to finally make contact.

The clouds began to creep into the periphery of the bowl. Vincent smiled like he would during an overture at the theater. He recited an incantation under his breath to further lure something to them.

"I see colors, mostly green," she said.

"Yes. Don't stop."

Her eyes flickered as she scanned every inch of reflective surface. "I feel something. A presence."

"Speak to it. Bring it forward." He continued his chanting.

She contorted her face, as if embarrassed to be speaking to a pool of wine. "I can see you. Let's talk." She held her breath as she waited.

Vincent couldn't take his eyes off her. His prayers became more passionate.

Her expression went blank, her face gray. Though she tried to hide it, the look of true fear crept into her eyes. "I am Margarite Duff," she stammered. "I speak for Vincent Croft." She focused intensely as she waited for a reply. Finally she looked at Vincent. "It says it has heard your calls."

Vincent was filled with genuine glee. His smile was so wide, his teeth seemed to eat his face. The months of dedication were not in vain. His feeble attempts to make contact had worked.

Rita's attention became focused again, then she translated what she'd heard. "It is aware of your intentions to become a Complete Man." She listened. *"That is quite the task."*

"Can it help me? Ask it if it will help me."

She asked the mirror. "Yes."

Vincent sighed in relief. He closed his eyes, one joyful tear dribbling down his cheek. "Ask how."

"How can he obtain your knowledge?" She thought for a second and added, "Without my assistance."

His first instinct was to be offended. What? Did she not enjoy spending time with him? Then he realized she was justified in asking such a question. He didn't want to rely on someone every time he needed to speak to them. The Complete Man needed to possess the ability to reach out to the other side whenever he wanted. To require the assistance of her would make him incomplete.

Rita shifted her eyes down and listened. Her eyebrows rose. She appeared surprised. Her face went soft as she looked at Vincent. "Gaze into the bowl and invite it in."

His mind flashed to teachings from his childhood. His parents dabbled in evocation of spirits. Actually, they more than dabbled; it was income, especially for his mother. For a period of about four years, she had clients come to the house for readings. These people were often sad, having recently lost a loved one or seeking advice from a ghost about romance. Rarely did anyone just want to chat with their dead sister or great-grandfather. Even with the most desperate of customers, his mother had taken precautions. There was a strict difference between evocation, which brought spirits forward, and invocation, which brought spirits inward. Evocation was safe; it kept the barrier between life and death intact. Invocation was risky because it blurred boundaries.

Never did she allow a spirit to manifest itself physically, say by inhabiting a toy or houseplant. Such actions would lead to a haunting. And she never invited a spirit to enter a human body. That brought the risk of possession. One way for a medium to control a spirit was to learn its name. This should be done immediately upon contact; before, if possible. In all the excitement of preparing for the ritual, he'd forgotten to instruct Rita on these things.

With the being so close, he was afraid to offend it by

communicating this to her. But he wasn't comfortable going in blind and doing something he'd been told his whole life not to do. So he spoke up. "First, I must ask your name. With whom are we speaking?"

Rita glanced down and waited. She looked back to him and shrugged.

"I mean no offense." He struggled to find a convincing reason to ask such a powerful question. "But if you are to be my new teacher, I must know what to call you."

Rita snapped her attention to the bowl. It was speaking. "You may call me *teacher*."

Vincent broke into a nervous sweat. "But your name. What is your given name?" He tried to breathe out his anxiety. Confidence was momentarily his. "If I'm to trust you, I must know this."

The flames of the candles once more changed size, growing and shrinking like lungs. Rita referred to the liquid mirror. After absorbing its information, she spoke. "I am a primordial being. I am older than time. At my creation, we had no names. So again, you may call me *teacher*."

Vincent could see a crossroad ahead of him. One way was cautious and well-traveled. He would decline the request and find another way to accomplish his goal. But this risked offending his...*teacher* and possibly many other beings with it. What if tonight was his only opportunity? He contemplated the other road. It was a risky one. Going down it would mean opening his life to this being and absorbing all it had to offer, good and bad.

But would it be bad? He knew Dark Magic, he'd studied it. Not for the sake of practicing, just to recognize it should it creep into his life. The ritual he was involved in wasn't evil. It was positive, simply about enlightenment. The knowledge he'd acquire would be used for good. Looking into that mirror would bring him everything he'd ever dreamed of.

The beginning of a new life started now.

❖

Vincent groaned as the morning sun woke him two hours before he pleased. He reached for a pillow to cover his head, but didn't find one. That bed only had one for him and one for Salvatore. Had they slept at his place, there'd be three extra pillows to pile on top of one another. Actually extra pillows weren't even necessary because he had heavy velvet hanging over the windows. Most people had curtains, blinds, shades, *something* to protect sleeping faces from sun, noise, and the elements. But not Salvatore. His windows were bare. Everything on God's green earth was permitted to blast through those thin panes of glass and assault Vincent when all he wanted to do was sleep in. He turned away from the harsh light, facing Sal.

Sal's eyes were closed. He smiled, reached for Vince's face, and patted his cheek. "It's okay. It's just sun."

"You're lucky I like you," Vince grumbled. "This would be intolerable otherwise."

Sal tried to laugh, but his voice hadn't totally woken up yet. "And you're lucky I like you. Your complaining would have had you kicked out months ago." He grinned once more, then moved closer to Vincent, burrowing his face into his chest. He let out a contented sigh.

Vincent held Sal tightly and rubbed his bare back. He looked around the room. The apartment wasn't very appealing. Flakes of dried white paint clung precariously to the uneven walls, some occasionally floating to the ground when there was too much movement in the room. The floors had been stripped of varnish and turned varying shades of brown and black, as wood does when it begins to decompose. And all four of those windows were as large as Cadillacs. If a person were to situate himself in front of them, the room seemed to have been built among the clouds. A crooked old piano sat there, perfect for Sal to lose himself in the view. That, Vincent assumed, was the reason Salvatore refused to put up window dressings and why he kept that decrepit apartment even though his salary allowed for something nicer. *Oh, artists*, he thought.

Then he had a clever idea, one that caused a devilish smirk to creep across his face. He discreetly whispered a commandment, raised his hand and waved it toward the foot of the bed. Very slowly, a tattered woven rug rose off the floor. He flicked his wrist in the direction of the group of windows, and the rug blocked out the rising sun. Vincent was pleased with his effort, so he tapped the air and spoke a word to keep in place.

Salvatore stirred and looked around the dimmed room. "How did you do that?"

Vincent chuckled. "It's a secret."

He sat up. "No, really. Vince, how are you doing this?"

"I told you. I've been learning."

Sal was quiet as he observed his rug mysteriously hanging in the air. "But this is impossible."

"Apparently not, if I'm doing it." He admired his handiwork. "The right words have power. And words combined with intention and gesture have more."

"How come you've never shown me this before?"

"I've only just learned the correct vocabulary. And this is only telekinesis. I'll soon do more than this. Much, much more." He mouthed a charm and waved his hand back and forth. The rug followed. He was pleased with himself. "Once

I've mastered my powers, I'll teach you. I'll teach everyone in the Circle."

Sal folded his arms as if he'd suddenly become cold. "Can you put it down?"

"Of course I can, but I want to sleep in without going blind."

Salvatore nudged him with his elbow. "But what's better than waking up with the sun?"

"Waking up next to your lover." Vincent paused. "Your lover who can do magic."

Sal erupted into laughter and cupped Vincent's face in his hands. He kissed him deeply, letting out gleeful noises every time he came up for breath. They rolled around in the rickety iron bed, exploring each other's warm skin with their hands and tongues.

Several times a certain nibble or stroke would send Vincent's mind reeling into ecstasy, into a place that seemed beyond this realm where only he and Sal existed. When that pleasure lured him away from reality, the rug would tremor or droop. A shaft of light would illuminate an elbow or a tuft of hair or pile of sheets, alerting him of the magic's fading. But it was nothing a quick commandment couldn't remedy.

Then abruptly, Sal went rigid. He sat up.

"What's wrong?" Vincent asked.

"Don't you taste that?"

"Taste what?" He licked his lips. "Damn." Vincent shook out his hand. The rug fell, fully bathing them in bright light.

A ghastly expression appeared on Sal's face, and he looked at the pillow. Vincent did too.

A puddle of blood pooled on the white sham, coming from his nose.

"Why is that happening?" Sal cried. "Vince, why is that happening?"

Vincent bolted up, tilting his head back to prevent more blood from flowing. "It's fine, it's fine. I think it's stopping." He hurried to the sink.

"But why? Did I hurt you?"

"No. Not at all. It must be the heat. It's dry in here. That must be it."

HAROLD

Autumn 1922

"There's a boathouse on the west side of the lake," Harold huffed. "Store it there. I don't know why I'm the one telling you how to do your job."

Leo C. wrinkled his brow. "Won't people be using it?" he asked.

Harold was normally a controlled kind of guy. Quiet and calm. But that thumb-shaped idiot really knew how to push his buttons. Stupid questions, over and over. "Not if you put a guy there with a gun in his jacket to tell everybody it's closed." Harold draped his overcoat on his arm and plopped his hat on his head. "You figure it out. Just tell me if you want it or not."

"It just sounds risky. I got cops on my ass because of what happened down south."

Harold gritted his teeth. "It's not the biggest resort town on the eastern seaboard, Leo. It's a hotel in the middle of the fucking woods. If a cop pulls up, I say pour them a glass. Congratulate him on not getting eaten by a bear on his way to arrest you."

"There ain't no bears in Jersey."

"I need to move this stuff by Friday. If you can't do that for me, I'll walk downtown and find another greasy Italian to do business with." Harold opened the door. "I expect a call tomorrow." He slipped into the hallway and made sure not to look back. That tough-guy act was strategic. And necessary. Harold had rehearsed several different versions of that conversation. Unfortunately he had to perform the one he was least looking forward to. He hated convincing people to do things. And negotiating was tedious. It'd be easiest if Leo simply accepted the offer or flat-out refused. The two ends of the spectrum were a breeze. That middle area was trying.

Even so, he knew Leo would agree to take the product. He always did. This song and dance happened every time, and besides, nobody else was making the guy offers. What other supplier would put the effort into personally traveling all the way down to that place? Nobody, that's who. The other guys were lazy, only selling to joints in the city. Not Harold Roth. He knew *everybody* was irked by this amendment, that people all over the place craved a drink, not just New Yorkers. So he built his empire in Jersey, Philly, and even parts of Delaware.

A man in an ill-fitting suit held the hotel door open while he passed through. "Have a safe trip home, Mr. Roth," he said. "I hope that Madelyn Vicks comes with you next time. She's a real beaut."

Harold pretended to laugh. "Don't get too attached. She's a taken lady, and you don't want any trouble from Mr. Croft." They shared a hearty chuckle, then Harold nodded, turned, and sighed an irritated sigh to himself.

The sun was setting and the humidity that made summer nights comfortable had retreated with the season. He decided to put on his overcoat. Still, two boats were being paddled around the man-made lake beside the hotel. A pair of lovers rowed one, and the other by a father whose little boy laughed when the oars came up from the water to splash him. Harold didn't like the thought of a child like that being denied a boat ride by one of Leo C.'s oafs.

Not my problem. He always had to remind himself that. The only thing he needed to be concerned about was moving the cases out of his basement. It was too risky to keep them there. And too expensive. Sitting on that much product was silly. Why hold on to it when it could be sold?

A deep, solid voice boomed from behind. "Mr. Roth!" Harold turned. A compact man with wavy black hair stood behind him. His suit was new and tailored perfectly for his squat build. He extended his right hand for a shake. "They call me Cooper. Can I have a moment of your time?"

Harold tried to hide his confusion. He'd never seen the man before. Still, he shook Cooper's hand. Something felt off about his grip. When the greeting was complete, he watched the man retract his hand. He was missing two fingers. "Ah... Roth. Harold Roth." He looked at his watch even though he was perfectly aware what time it was. "Just a minute. I should be getting back to the city."

"I understand," said Cooper. "I'll be doing the same after I deal with Leo here. What an oaf, huh?" He laughed. "I live in Hoboken. I run several *businesses* around there."

Harold's chest tightened. He'd heard of a new boss across the river in Jersey. Rumor had it that this guy was ruthless, that he'd taken out the previously reigning establishment, a whole family, without any warning. He saw opportunities and simply seized them. No negotiations needed. Just a gun and a shovel. That man didn't play by any rules. Roth tried to say something, but everything he thought of could easily seem suspicious. Instead, he decided on seeking clarity. "I, ah... didn't know Leo C. had a business partner down here."

Cooper laughed again, this time without even opening his

mouth. It sounded more like a growl than anything. "Let's just say he does now. I'm branching out. So that means we'll soon be business partners." He smiled. His teeth were perfectly white and straight and menacing.

Harold's hands trembled. He hid them behind his back and nodded. "Then I'm happy to make your acquaintance."

"And on behalf of Leo C., I'm happy to take you up on your offer."

"That's wonderful. I can get the order down here by next week."

"Good. Good." He took out a cigar, stuck it between his pearly whites, and spoke out the corner of his mouth. "And I want to double the order for my place up north."

Harold's eyes widened with genuine glee. He didn't want to appear too excited because that was weak, but goddamn that was a huge order with an equally huge payout. "Yes. Yes, of course."

Cooper reached into his coat pocket and produced an overstuffed envelope. "Here. Take this to know I'm a serious man."

Harold retrieved it with his shaky hand. "Thank you, Mr. Cooper."

"Just Cooper. No mister necessary."

"Of course." Harold thought the name was odd for someone with such an olive complexion. "That's, um…an English name, yes?"

"It is." Cooper took out an impressive lighter and ignited a flame for the end of his giant cigar. He blew out a puff of smoke once the cherry was appropriately hot. "Yet I am not an English person. I'm quite mixed, actually. A mutt. But you see, I think names are important. So, if I come across a person I don't like with a good name, I take it. I flaunt it for a while until it becomes better, and the old bearer of that name is forgotten. I call it legacy work." He sucked on the cigar once more and exhaled an even larger cloud than before. As soon as the smoke cleared and their faces were once again visible, he spoke. "Make sure you come through for me. Roth is a good name. Don't force me to make it better."

They said their good-byes and made arrangements for product to be distributed on specific dates. Harold wasn't thrilled about making deals with such a volatile man, but he wasn't worried. He had the stock and soon he'd have the money to get even more. If he just complied with what Cooper wanted, he'd be fine. He'd be rich. Well, richer.

Roth's driver, Jim, opened the car door for him. "Perfect timing, sir. I may just have you back by dinner."

Harold smiled and ducked into the backseat. They pulled away quickly for their journey north. Harold's favorite part of traveling to and from that place was looking out the window. The Grand Pines Hotel was a twelve-story art deco behemoth that stuck up from the forest like a mountain. Watching its main tower appear above the canopy as he arrived and disappear in the distance as he journeyed home was a magical experience, something he thought a person could only see in far-off European lands where castles still stood in enchanted woods.

It would take just a few hours at most to get back to the estate, and the first thing he planned on doing was calling on Clarissa. It had been a long trip and he needed some familiar company. The women he'd encountered while away were nice. Well, some not so nice, but they nonetheless provided some enjoyment. Being a man of means, especially a man in his field, created expectations. People wanted to see him with a harem at his heels, a wife and five mistresses, or a minor celebrity in every city. But he didn't partake in such indulgences.

When he first struck it big a year and a half earlier, he tried that. It wasn't his style. He simply didn't have the appetite for such lavishness. Residing in that airship hangar of a house was bad enough. He'd only purchased it to keep up appearances. Seemed like the right thing to do, even though he was more content in a small apartment. That was how he was raised. He found it funny that the extravagant homes and multiple women and endless power he yearned for while growing up in that shoebox actually made him uncomfortable. So on nights when most millionaires would want to paint the town gold arm in arm with every celebrity from there to Timbuktu, Harold desired to simply be at home in the company of one nice person.

The car pulled up to the mansion, where all the old familiar lights were glowing in the windows. The housekeeper must have come in and made the place welcoming even though Harold had told her not to bother. As he passed through the entry, he spoke with authority. "I appreciate you being here, but as I said, it really isn't necessary." He laid his hat and coat on a table at the bottom of the stairs. "Please take the rest of the evening off. I'm receiving a guest in about an hour, and we can manage quite nicely alone." He started up the stairs to change.

"You have a fine staff," said someone from the parlor doorway.

Startled, Harold turned. "Oh, Vincent," he said. He clutched his heart and exhaled. "It's you." He smiled and stepped down three steps toward him. "I was expecting to hear the housemaid's voice. Yours is quite different." He chuckled. Vincent wasn't joining him, he just stood in the middle of the foyer and fidgeted with his hands. "What's the matter? Why are you here?"

Vincent's focus was elsewhere. "The Circle was..." He lost himself in a thought.

Harold cautiously stepped down to meet him. "It was weeks ago, yes?"

Vincent snapped to attention. "During the full moon," he said. He nervously played with the buttons on his cardigan.

Harold peered at him suspiciously. "I must assume it went well. The show's reviews are good. Business, too. But it can always be better." He laughed, and thought for a moment. "Was Missy there? She'd felt a tickle in her throat last we spoke. I hope you were able to focus on fixing that."

"She wasn't," said Vincent. He struggled to speak before finally blurting, "It wasn't a full Circle, Roth."

Harold's grin froze. "What does that mean? You need to have at least four members to do the rituals. What did you do instead? Three of you sit around with candles and a spirit board?"

"Two of us. We didn't do the rituals. We did an evocation." He studied his fingernails. "*The* evocation."

Any vestiges of glee he'd felt from his friend's surprise greeting diminished. "You know how I feel about that, Vince."

"And you know how I feel. It's important to me. To the Circle."

"Our coven was supposed to be equal. No supreme ruler or priest or whatever mumbo-jumbo you call it."

"You know that can't work. These things need leaders, real leaders who can elevate the group. I've always had more abilities. I've studied this my whole life. If I develop, we can move beyond these *simple* spells."

"These simple spells have given us all great advantages in our fields, in our lives."

Vincent chuckled and shook his head. "*Help me get a raise* and *heal my ankle* and *don't let the cops see me.* Easy. I can do those in my sleep. And without hearing everyone cluck about how exciting it is to see candles smoke a little more than they should. I am...*we* are capable of greater things."

Harold was quiet, deciding to focus on the crown molding above Vincent's head to keep calm. "Well, then how did it go?" he finally asked, almost in a whisper. "Do you feel *enlightened*? Are you *advancing*?"

"Yes." His words were separated and clipped. "Greatly. Every day."

"Fantastic. I'm happy for you." He turned. "I've had a long journey. I need to retire." He ascended the stairs. "Jim is outside if you need a ride to the station."

"But it didn't come without cost."

Harold froze. He dug his fingernails into the banister, scraping up its waxy finish. His mind raced with possibilities of what that cost could be. Did he give up blood or a limb or somebody's firstborn? That was what happened in literature, at least. He turned to face him again.

"As I said," began Vincent. "Your staff is very nice. Helpful. The evocation had to be performed in a specific place. Your basement was ideal. There was an incident."

Harold's eyes swirled with anger and horror and fear. "Tell me."

Vincent's hands and voice shook. "When the veil between worlds was finally parted, when the spirit was invited here, its power was great. I had no idea with what force it would arrive." He rolled up his sleeve. Gruesome gray-yellow bruises covered his forearm.

"Christ. What happened?"

"It was an explosion of sorts. A blast. I'm fine. We are fine."

Harold was able to breathe. Relief. "Thank goodness."

"But your inventory is another story."

His throat closed again, catching anger in the space between his eyes. "How much of it?"

"Nearly half. It's all been cleaned. Looks nicer down there than it did when we arrived."

"You have no idea what you've done." Harold stepped down with precision. "That product is my livelihood." He stopped and took hold of the railing. "*Our* livelihood." He leaned over the banister and panted as he spoke. "And now there's only what...half to move? Half to *sell*? You're leaving me in the hole, Vince. You think the people in this business are kind? You think they'll understand when I tell them some fuck-up dandy blew their incomes to smithereens while playing with his magic wand?" He roared and grabbed Vincent's shoulders, shaking him to communicate how disastrous this was. "This is bad!"

Vincent pushed him away. "Relax." Harold flew into the wall with more force than a simple push should cause. "I'll fix it."

Harold groaned as he found his footing. "How? How can you fix this? Turn back time? Reassemble every broken bottle and ferment new booze to fill them with?"

"I screwed up. I'm sorry. But soon it'll be worth it."

"No. It won't. You're a loose cannon, pal. I don't trust you or your theoretical powers. Even if you have some, you'll never learn how to harness them. You're a wannabe." He hobbled up toward the landing.

Vincent murmured a spell and waved his hand to lock Harold's legs. With the twirl of a finger and a flick of his wrist, he turned Harold around and pinned him to the wall. Vincent unblinkingly held him in his gaze as he floated two inches off the floor. He whispered an incantation that brought Harold to him.

"What was that you said, pal?" Vincent smirked, showing just a few menacing teeth. "If it weren't for me, you'd have forty stab wounds in your back, bleeding on the floor of a prison shower. The Feds were this close to nabbing you for all those shady deals. I got you outta that mess. I performed the rites, I did the conjuring, I created the—"

"You think this magic of yours gives you power?" Harold coughed. "Bullshit. You know what gives people power? Money. And I've got lots of it. So much so that you would be nothing if not for me and my money. I'm pumping it into your show, into your publicity, into making everyone think you're engaged to Miss Vicks when we all know you're munching on teacakes with the piano player. Your magic might be able to do some tricks. Cover up some bad deals and bring you and this coven some small favors, small favors that *yes* I'm thankful for, but you better remember your place. I have the green. I control your green. And green is the only thing that really matters."

Vincent's face reddened with hot anger. An emerald hue seeped into his eyes. He inhaled deeply into his diaphragm and then released a wretched, guttural screech.

The scream took shape as words, every one of them tightening around Harold's neck as if a rope were slowly being pulled taut around it.

Footsteps clamored through the empty halls, followed by a voice. "Stop it!" Rita came running in. She put her hand on Vincent's shoulder and pulled him back. "Leave him alone."

Vincent blinked twice, returning his irises to their normal blue. He shook his head and then appeared to register what he'd been doing. He put his hands up, like he'd been held at gunpoint.

Harold tumbled to the ground, holding his throat with one hand while he gasped for air and pointed at Vincent with the other. "You pull another stunt like that…" He coughed. "I'll have you yanked outta that show so fast your head will fall off." He coughed again. "Then I'll put a bullet in it."

❖

The men stumbled into the study. It was a respectable room with tall windows, taller bookshelves, and a collection of exotic game trophies displayed above the fireplace. Vincent stared cross-eyed at a gazelle. "Hello, madame," he said with a bow.

"I bought her…no, wait. Maybe she's a him. Antlers and such." Harold stepped toward the head and scrunched his face in thought. "Whatever she is, I bought it from a very nice African man uptown. He has quite a collection."

Rita hollered from the hallway. "This bottle is officially empty!" She stepped into the room and immediately locked her eyes on the gazelle in front of Harold's face. "Oh, this is depressing. We can't drink in here."

"It's not depressing," Vincent said. "It's esteemed. And one cannot sit in such an esteemed-looking room without an equally esteemed-looking drink in hand." He slid to the butler bar and held up a crystal decanter.

Harold rushed to his side. "That one might be a little too esteemed-looking, friend." He reached for a bottle and struggled to read the label.

"Whatever that is, I'm not going to drink it," said Rita. "I don't drink brown liquor. Gets me all zozzled."

Vincent threw his long arms around her. "She's been so patient with us. Watching us argue like two schoolboys. Give the lady a nice bottle of bubbles."

Rita's face lit up. "Yes, let's toast to friendship."

"I'll fetch it." Vincent ran out of the room.

"It will be in the corner of the basement you didn't destroy!" Harold laughed. He turned to Rita. Her cheeks were flushed from drinking, making the shadows in her dimples appear more pronounced. He gazed at her for a moment too long, then cleared his throat.

She giggled and walked to the Victrola. "I'm glad you two made up."

"Vincent and I are very good at arguing. Fortunately we're just as good at reconciliation." He noticed her eyeing the machine. "Music?"

"That'd be lovely."

As he wound the key, he noticed the unmarked record on the turntable. "You might recognize this one." He released the brake and allowed the record to spin. Finally, he placed the needle down and allowed a fox-trot to pour into the room.

"Harold, it's wonderful." She admired the machine. "I imagine little men inside with tiny horns. Maybe pygmies you picked up on your travels."

He grinned, a little too tickled and drunk to try and reply with words. Even after their laughter had subsided and she was doing nothing of interest, just bouncing her head to the music, he found himself still smiling. She had a quality that made him feel as if she'd been around forever, an old friend in the body of someone he'd just recently met. She was eager to jump into virtually any conversation, whether it involved her or not. She wasn't shy about voicing her opinion or asking someone else to elaborate on theirs. He'd grown up with energy like hers. Children, especially young girls in his tenement, were like that. Fathers and brothers had to be rough and tough to get by, so mothers and daughters followed suit. Being the delicate flower society expected would only lead to trouble. Rita, like his mother and his sister, had a fierce presence.

A snare drum rattled from the Victrola, followed by Sing

Sing Walker's bass voice. Rita perked up when she heard the first lyrics to last year's big hit. "You devil!" she said. She tapped her feet against the bare floor. "This song is from our rival show."

"But Mr. Walker is not himself our enemy," Harold said. "He's a member of the Circle."

"I'm no dummy. I saw him there." She ran her fingers around the rim of a champagne coupe. "I just didn't realize you were such an avid supporter of shows I'm not in." She smirked.

"How could a person not indulge in a talent like that?" asked Vincent from the doorway. He had two bottles in his hand. "That's the kind of man who should headline." He looked sadly at nothing in particular. "It's…it's just not right, that's what." He hiccupped. "That cellar gives me the creeps."

Harold disregarded him with a wave. "I'm a man of little talent." He tried to walk in time toward Rita. "See, I can't even walk on a beat." They laughed. "But I find talent oh so beguiling." He locked eyes with her and turned up the corners of his mouth.

"That explains your fascination with Clarissa," Rita said. She winked, picked up a glass, and tapped over to Vincent. "Tell me, will you use your new gifts to exalt deserving men like Mr. Walker to unfathomable fame?"

"I don't know about that," Vincent said. He popped the cork and held his bottle to his chin as he thought. "But I will do something for him and his kind. And for mine."

Harold and Rita shared a look. *His kind?*

Vincent caught on and elaborated. "Those of us with gifts mustn't squander our power on selfish acts. That's been done by too many men. Where are the powerful now?" He poured champagne into Rita's glass. "We meet secretly in attics and basements."

"He fancies himself a liberator," someone said from the doorway. Clarissa sauntered in, dressed in a long white robe and a turban clipped with a jeweled butterfly.

Harold bolted to her side. "Angel!" They kissed. She wasn't wearing much makeup. She looked soft. He preferred her this way.

Vincent blew her a kiss. "You look ravishing, my dear."

Clarissa nodded and looked seriously to Rita. "With Vincent, the world will evolve. It will accept your family, my family, and his family. And if it doesn't, we will make it." Her face lit up, her eyes sparkling like that brooch on her turban. She ran to Rita with outstretched arms. "Good to see you here."

❖

"Mama practiced magic in the cemetery with the other women."

"I had an obvious advantage being brought up that way."

"My aunt brought me to one as a child. I think about it every day."

"I'm a methodical man. I enjoy the ritual. Luckily, we've seen results from that."

"Everyone in New Orleans does it. It's inescapable."

"I knew there was a spirit in that house. I could feel it as young as eight years old."

"I think it frightened her. We never spoke about it."

"This guy over here is the one with talent. I'm just support."

"They strung him up. She was afraid they'd find a reason to do the same to her, so she stopped. We all did."

"I only think he does it because I do. He's such a cynic, but I adore him."

"He says it's inevitable. One day I'll be like that lady."

"I was in a rough spot, and he helped me. Well, his knowledge of all this *stuff* did."

"Most bodies still move even after the head is lopped off. That's when the magic is greatest. That's what Mama said."

"Did you see that?"

"You trust him so much? I don't. Maybe it's the champagne talking, but I don't."

"But you're beautiful. Nobody ever told you that?"

"Two years ago. At a party, just like you. I wandered upstairs, and here I am now."

"I'm sorry. I haven't been myself lately."

"Sometimes I wonder if it's our place or not."

"You're beautiful, too, darling. You know that."

"I didn't know there was any doubt."

"He gets offended if I don't make time for him."

"I could ask her."

By three in the morning, nobody was listening to anybody, just spouting theories and opinions that only made sense in their heads. Vincent had sprawled out across a chaise and fallen asleep with an empty glass in his hand. Harold and Clarissa cuddled on one end of a long couch, her head on his shoulder. Rita sat on the other. She stirred a glass of champagne with her fingertip, watching the bubbles rise and fall. Her fingernail clinked the glass, frightening her. She glanced at Harold to see if she'd disturbed him. He stared back at her. He'd been watching her for several minutes already. "I should be home by now," she said. "There's a show tomorrow."

"Jimmy's shift ended hours ago," he whispered. "The train stopped running until morning. You're stuck here with us characters." Vincent shifted in his sleep, twitched and flailed. He breathed heavily and made sounds like he was having a nightmare. Rita started to shake him, but Harold stopped her. "No, no. Leave him."

"But he's frightened."

Clarissa groaned. He patted her head to relax her and changed his voice to an even softer whisper. "Sometimes what we call during our rituals is manifested in our dreams. Visions. We must let them speak to us."

Rita helplessly gazed at Vincent. She shuddered. "Does that mean the spirit we called is in his head or in this room with us?"

"I'm not sure. I haven't done this sort of ritual before."

She glanced at a mirror over the mantel. She adjusted her body away from it and spoke into her lap. "I'm worried about him."

Harold didn't like watching her retreat like that. He wished he could see her eyes. "Why?"

She looked at Vincent, to the mirror, and then back to her lap. "He told me he's been seeing things."

"I should hope so." He quietly laughed. "That's what he wanted. The two of you blew up my basement to make it happen."

She strained to speak clearly. "And I sometimes wish I hadn't."

"It's helping him. He's gaining the power he's wanted."

Rita finally looked at him. Her cheeks were painted black from running mascara. "At what cost?" She crumbled.

Harold reached for Rita's hand, trying not to disrupt Clarissa on his shoulder. All he could touch were the ends of her fingers, but he still tried to give them a comforting squeeze. She half laughed at his effort and tried to smile. That was when their eyes made contact. Since the day he met her, he'd been hypnotized by those large, green eyes. He reckoned that was why she was becoming such a popular entertainer. Everyone was enamored by them. Those eyes could be seen from the last row at the top of the house. What looked like permanent dark circles under them made the white parts glisten from just about any distance. The result, at least according to one review that Harold saved in his desk drawer, was a "perpetually open quality to Miss Duff that draws the audience into her scenes, causing them to never want to leave." Ever since that write-up, Harold yearned for her company more and more.

Rita quietly gasped and withdrew her hand.

Harold felt Clarissa's head rise. "Mr. Roth," she began, "you should have said something earlier. I'm all groggy now."

He fell over his words. "I'm…what are you talking about?"

Clarissa stood. "I might have an hour left in me, but that's about it." She smoothed her dress and looked squarely at Rita. "Come on."

They stared blankly at her.

Clarissa raised her eyebrows. "Harold, I know you think she's pretty. I think she's pretty, too. So…"

Rita turned red. "Are you suggesting we…a…"

"You've never done this before, have you?" Rita was silent. It didn't seem possible for her to blush any more, but she did. "It's okay, chickadee. It'll be fun."

❖

The birds waking up outside the window announced sunset was approaching. Harold liked few things less than falling asleep as the world woke up, but he decided not to fixate on that. Instead he'd relax and think about how unexpectedly wonderful the evening had been. A chuckle escaped him while he replayed the extreme highs and lows of the last several hours. The laugh was a bit too loud. He glanced at the ladies on either side of him to see if he'd woken them, but they were fast asleep. Clarissa lay on her back, her face toward him. She looked just like a magazine illustration of a sleeping woman, a hand effortlessly placed on the pillow, pointing to her slightly parted lips. Rita was on her stomach, absconding with one of the bed's many pillows. Her face also faced his, but in a less picturesque way. Her open mouth and exhausted expression made him smile.

As sleep began to melt his thoughts, a creaking roused him back to consciousness. He raised his head to see Vincent standing in the doorway. He was nearly panting. "May I join you?" he asked. His teeth chattered.

With wide eyes, Harold looked at the two barely covered women next to him and then back to Vincent. He shook his head. "No."

Vincent looked behind him and then tiptoed inside. "I can't be alone right now." A few steps closer, and Harold saw he was drenched in sweat, pale as the sheets the threesome was wrapped in. Harold watched his friend crawl to the end of the bed and curl up like an animal at their feet.

"Vince. What's wrong?"

Vincent's body heaved. A series of silent sobs escaped him.

❖

To Harold, the round table in the room with olive walls was not only practical, but symbolic. Like the knights of Camelot, the members of their Circle were equal when they sat around it. So when Vincent suggested the layout of the room be altered, Harold was reluctant. But battling with Vincent on any subject was futile. Somehow he always convinced his opponent he was right. Maybe it was his God-given charm or maybe it was his newfound power. Whatever the reason, Harold eventually caved in and allowed him to remove the table and replace it with rows of chairs, a classroom in which Vincent could teach his friends what he'd learned.

During Vincent's seminar, members of the Circle were enthusiastic about jumping to the front of the class to assist in demonstrating his exotic spells. A dancer named Shelly made sheets of paper rise and fall with a word and a flick of her index finger, Clarissa moved water from one glass into another with just a simple charm and a strategic blink, and Sing Sing caused the wind to blow with a hymn and a whistle. With the transference of every piece of knowledge, Vincent became more and more excited. He was never a humble man, but all sense of modesty vanished as he very clearly realized the power he had, not just as a magician, but as a teacher. That, Harold feared, was more dangerous than any spell Vincent could learn from an otherworldly being. The influence he had on the group was becoming apparent. Harold hoped it would be a positive one.

He hated thinking negatively about his friend. He knew Vince only performed that song and dance to help his fellow man, to elevate the Circle and give power to those who had none. He tried to focus on the good happening in that room, but it was difficult. His mind was on more ominous matters, like the loss of the majority of his stock in the basement. His clients, especially Cooper, were seeking product, and he didn't have enough to deal out. The very thought of breaking the news to them made him break out in a cold sweat. No, more than that. It made him want to run away to Mexico to seek sanctuary in a church nobody knew about. So finding anything positive about…well, *anything* was an arduous task.

"Who's next?" Vincent asked, scanning the room. "Somebody new who hasn't been up here yet." He skipped over several raised hands and landed on Salvatore, whose body language suggested anything but a desire to participate. "Salvatore. How about we make some fire?"

Sal's expression was blank. "I'm fine, thank you," he said. Then he crossed his legs and turned his head to the wall.

Vincent tossed his hair back. "He's always been afraid of attention. Come now."

"Really, Vince. I'm quite content observing."

"Darling, show everyone how much fun you are."

Sal shot Vince a look that could cut diamonds.

Vincent rolled his eyes, moaned a Latin phrase, and swooped his hand through the air. Sal's chair launched him forward, forcing him to stand or fall.

"That's not fair," Sal said. He stumbled over his tangled legs. "You can't force me to do this."

"Oh, stop being such a wet blanket and get up here." Vincent clapped and urged the rest of the group to join him. They did. Sal eventually became embarrassed and stomped to the front. He put up his hands like a criminal surrendering to the police and urged the applause to cease. Vincent subtly guided him by placing his hand on the small of his back. "There you go. Now you're on the trolley."

Sal tried to keep a sour face, but a chuckle escaped him. "I usually stay in the orchestra pit for a reason."

Vincent crumpled the same papers Shelly had levitated and threw them in a pile on the floor. "Now, with concentration, a gesture, and some magic words, we will make a little bonfire."

Harold perked up. "Not too big, I hope," he said. "Some of us live here."

Vincent shook his head and smiled. "My pupil here isn't

quite experienced enough to burn down the house." He looked at Sal. "It'll be like lighting a candle."

Sal raised an eyebrow and crossed his arms. "Who says I can't do more?"

"Because I haven't taught you more, that's why." Vince cleared his throat. "Now fire, just like the wind Sing Sing conjured, has a name. By calling upon this name, we can control it."

"So we can't do magic without speaking? There's no way to manipulate elements without using a name?"

"That's correct," said Vincent. He turned to his audience. "At least that's how I've been taught." He laughed and so did they.

Salvatore had a sinister, challenging smirk painted on his face. Harold was tickled by their tension. Sometimes lovers enjoyed pressing each other's buttons just as much as enemies.

"Focus on the papers," Vincent said. "Imagine heat building there. Charge the spot with intention." The room was silent as Sal locked his eyes in place. His breathing was shallow and slow. "Now call upon the fire with its true name." Vincent looked back to the class. "These names are sacred, ones that I was authorized to learn. Now I entrust you, my friends, with them." He whispered the ancient word into Sal's ear, then raised his voice for all to hear. "Say it aloud for all to know."

Sal did as instructed. As soon as the sound left his lips, the energy of the room changed. Harold instinctually loosened his collar. Had it become warmer?

"Now," Vincent said, "the gesture." He rubbed his thumb and middle finger together. "Kindle it."

Sal raised his hand and performed the same motion. A crackle sounded. A spark flew. His attention remained fixed on the paper, and he continued to rub his fingers. Vincent was nodding enthusiastically. Sal spoke the name once more, this time louder. Suddenly, a flame rose from the floor. It was a giant, roaring creation of about five feet tall.

The members in the first row jolted to their feet, practically leaping over their chairs to escape. Everyone screamed.

"No!" yelled Salvatore. He stepped in front of Vincent and spread his arms. His eyes widened, and he stared at the base of the flame like a wild animal would at its prey. He spoke softly and intensely. "No." The fire immediately shrunk, as if it'd been extinguished with a bucket of water.

As everyone tried to recover from the fright, Harold watched the magician and his assistant at the front. Vincent's face was pale. He grabbed Salvatore's hand. When Sal turned to look at him, Vincent said, "Thank you." He seized Sal's face and passionately kissed him on the lips.

The session ended shortly after that. Harold stood in the back of the room as everyone filed out. Rita peeked her head through the doorway. "I didn't see you here before," he said.

Rita moved to the side to allow someone through. "I watched from the hall."

He wrinkled his brow. "Whatever for?"

"Trying to avoid mirrors like that." She tilted her head to reference the gilded mirror in the corner. "Gives me the creeps. Never know what you'll see in them."

"I could have it removed for you."

She held up her finger. "Don't worry about me."

He couldn't help but grin. Even though the fire had gone out, he still felt warm. "Would you like to stay for a drink?"

Rita gazed deeply into his eyes and then looked at away, at Clarissa. She was standing on the other side of the room talking with Missy. "I shouldn't," she said sadly. "I had fun.

But I don't want to tear focus from what you two have." She paused and searched for words. "And I fear if we continue, I'd want to be the focus. That's not possible or decent to do right now."

Harold nodded. "Right. That's respectable." Someone tapped on his shoulder. He whipped around and growled at the interrupter.

Vincent backed away. "I'm disrupting something?"

"No," said Rita. "I'm leaving." She looked to Harold, warmly. "Thank you for having us today." She walked away.

Harold placed a hand on his forehead and turned to the wall. "What do you want, Vince?"

"I was coming to apologize for almost burning your house down." He looked around and moved in to speak softer. "That wasn't supposed to happen. Sometimes I think these spells are exalting me, and sometimes I think they're threatening my life. Honestly, if Sal hadn't been there, you'd have a man with a melted face headlining the show."

Harold exhaled and looked to the ceiling. He opened his eyes wide to dry them.

"Roth, are you upset?"

"I'm just under a lot of stress," he said, shaking his head. He caught a glimpse of Clarissa. She winked at him. His chest became tight. "Sometimes life presents options and you wish you could live all of them, you know?"

Vincent hummed as he thought. "No. I think it's tough enough living one life, thank you very much."

"Fair." Harold rubbed the back of his neck to relieve some tension. "I also have this guy in Hoboken who is waiting on some barrels. Paid up front. But I simply don't have anything to give him." He glared at Vince to communicate whose fault that was.

"Oh, that."

"He's not the kind of guy you want to mess around with, if you know what I'm saying."

"He's dangerous?"

Harold gave one sarcastic chuckle. "That's putting it kindly. This guy is downright treacherous."

Vincent crossed his arms, grabbed his bottom lip, and thought. "I'll take care of it."

"What? Are you going to hocus pocus a few barrels into existence?"

"I'm the reason you're in this mess, and I'm going to get you out."

MADELYN

Winter 1923

Kansas felt like a world away. Maybe that was why Madelyn hadn't been back since she arrived in New York two years earlier. When her co-stars would ask why she'd never gone back to visit, she'd blame the long trip. "Have you been in transit for almost an entire day? It's enough to send a person straight to the nuthouse," she said. Everyone would laugh at her response, unaware of the sadness she was shielding. The truth was she desperately wanted to go home, but she couldn't.

The town of Salina had grown rapidly. First came the railroad, then the steam-powered mills and, most recently, the arrival of various forms of agriculture. A map of the area would look like a patchwork quilt of properties constantly battled over by big families and even bigger companies. Grampa managed to hold tightly to the Vicks farm, a modest patch of golden land crowned by a sprawling, mismatched house. The original structure had been built back when Kansas was settled, with room after room added as the family grew. They all lived there. They all worked there. They all were very close.

When Madelyn announced her aspirations to move to the big city, they laughed at her. "You ain't never seen a building over three stories tall," her father said. "You might fall over dead at the sight of one." He lit his pipe and made his way to the porch. "You'll do fine singing in the church. Dance at a social. A city like New York will chew you up and spit you out."

The men in her family weren't particularly mean, but their belief that her talents and desires were no more important than the family dog's made her hate them. Salina would chew her up, but unlike New York, it wouldn't spit her out. It'd hold her in its teeth until she became rot. Just like her mama and Aunties and long-dead Granny. The Vicks women were hardened, twisted things. She couldn't let that happen. So early one morning, she snuck into that drawer that nobody knew she knew about and took the money she needed to escape.

After she hit it big, she sent money home, lots of it every month. She'd paid back what she stole ten times over again. But they never returned her letters or made the visits she'd promised to pay for. She'd orphaned herself. More and more she began to feel like that, especially over the last several months. Like Daddy predicted, New York was beginning to clench its jaw on her. The pressure was tightest during her staged social affairs.

"I hate wearing this thing," she said. "It's too heavy." She raised her left hand to admire the giant diamond on her finger. "It is pretty, though."

"Maddy, it's just a few hours. When you're home, you can take it off." Harold shifted in the seat to look out the window of their car.

"If it doesn't burn a hole through my finger first." She scowled at Vincent next to her.

"Don't get sanctimonious on us, honey," he said. "Would

you rather break off the engagement?" He thought for a moment. "Of course, that would make quite a buzz. Get some attention."

"No," Harold interjected, still looking out the window. "It'd upset your chemistry onstage. One of you'd have to leave the show."

That made Madelyn shut her mouth. She knew if one of them was to depart, it'd have to be her. *Pretty blond girlies*, as Weinstein once called actresses like her, were swimming all over Broadway. They could just as easily pluck a replacement from the pool should she cause a stir. And Vincent, for some reason, was everybody's favorite. They'd never cut the cord with him.

"All right. I think I see one," Harold said. "No, there're two! Two cameras!" He turned to them. "You know the drill. And don't forget to mention the new Ali Baba number we're debuting next month."

"How could I forget?" she asked. "I thought that's why you dragged me out tonight. I'm not even in the mood to go to dinner."

Harold leaned in close. "We're doing this because the public loves you. Now go give them what they want."

The car door opened, soaking them in enough bright white flashes to cover up every one of their lies.

❖

She liked her new couch. It was gold, but not that dingy kind used on the fringe of curtains. This was a bright gold. Like a sunflower. No, like wheat. *Damn*, she thought. *Just like home.* She began to wonder if she'd ever escape that strange desire to be there again. To feel the flat earth beneath her feet. People don't often think of New York being hilly, but it is. Sometimes walking up an avenue felt like climbing a mountain, at least to a girl from Kansas. Her body was accustomed to even ground. Those hills hurt her back.

Even if the color of her new couch was a relic from her past, the piece of furniture itself was brand new, like nothing her family would ever be able to own. Sometimes she'd just stare at it. Admire it. If she sat on it for too long, she feared it'd look worn. She hated when things appeared old. Everything in her life was that way before coming to New York.

A desire bubbled in her. She wanted a drink. She'd never had one before. It was illegal. Sure, practically everyone did it anyway, but she didn't like the idea of breaking the law. Still, she was interested in sampling. Just indulging in that first sip, the one she'd so often witnessed others take. She carefully observed how quickly their nerves would settle when their throat muscles relaxed after swallowing, how the breath would be forced from their mouths. Ecstasy. If those moments were heaven, later ones seemed like hell. The stumbling, the anger, the foolishness, the lowered inhibitions—that stuff was frightening. Just knowing those effects lurked inside every open bottle was enough to scare her away from ever falling into temptation and taking even the tiniest of sips.

Her thoughts of drunkenness were interrupted by a real, live drunk. "Maddy," Vincent called. "Let me in." He pounded on the door with more force than a person should use after eleven o'clock. "We need to talk."

She cracked the door, careful to ensure the chain was still in place to keep it from fully opening. Her performance began with a yawn, rubbing her eyes with her hands. "Vincent, please. It's late."

"I'm sorry. I just need to…" He looked behind him, the tail of his sentence swallowed by the hallway.

"You're drunk."

"No shit."

"I'm going to bed. I'll see you tomorrow at rehearsal. Go home and sober up so you can be on time." She closed the door, secured the chain, and leaned against it. She waited to hear his footsteps retreat.

It was quiet. She put her ear to the door.

Whispering.

She struggled to understand. Out the corner of her eye, she saw the chain on the door tremble. She blinked twice, hoping it was maybe just a trick of the light, but when she glanced at it again, the chain slid quickly to the side and fell out of place. The door opened.

Vincent pushed through. "I'm sorry, I need to—"

"No!" she screamed, trying to slam the door closed.

But he was stronger. *Thump.* She flew across the room. Before she could crash into the side of her brand-new couch, her body came to a full stop. She was dangling six inches above the ground, held by a force that seemed to be tied around her limbs and puppeteered by the man who'd just broken in. Vincent stood five feet away with his hands over his head. They were filthy, covered in a brown crust. As he lowered his arms, she noticed the cuff of his shirt was stained a deep red. She descended at the same speed as his hands. Her back met the ground softly, like she'd been laid there by a lover.

"I don't mean to be a brute," he said, turning back to the door. He mumbled and waved his hand, slamming it. "And I don't want to cause alarm."

It was too late for that. Madelyn had crawled into a corner like a farm animal chosen for that night's supper. He already had somebody's blood on his hands and hers couldn't be next.

"Maddy, you need to help me." He crouched on the floor next to her. His jacket smelled like it'd been the victim of several spilled bottles of cologne and booze. "Salt! Where's the kitchen?" He bolted up and scanned the room for a doorway. When he found one, he zoomed toward it and tore through cabinets.

Madelyn slid up the wall, trembling. "You need to tell me what's going on." She spotted the phone on the table near her golden couch. "I'll call the police if you're in danger." Still more clamoring from the kitchen. "Or are you involved in something that'll get you in trouble?"

Just as she was about to make a move to the table, Vincent reappeared with a white enamel jar. She plastered herself safely back against the wall. He stuck as much of his bloodstained hand inside as he could and scooped out a mound of salt. He sprinkled it in front of the door.

She was so scared she thought she might vomit. She desperately searched for something she could say to stop him. "Vincent, I just had the place cleaned yesterday."

He turned around, eyes blazing green. "I need to do this!" he yelled. He marked the windows just as he had the door. Sweat surged from his pores, soaking his usually perfect hair into wild tendrils that seemed to want off his head as badly as Madelyn wanted out of that room. She abandoned the idea of going for the phone and instead concentrated on running out the door. But he was moving so quickly, so erratically that she couldn't find the opportunity. "That should do it," he said, trying to place the jar on the sill. His hands were shaking, and he had trouble getting it to rest. The canister rattled out of his grasp and spilled out on her rug. A wet, tear-soaked moan poured from him. "I don't want to bring you into this."

Madelyn squealed softly, frightfully. "I don't understand what you're saying." She slowly crept to the door as he wept. "But I'm going to get some help."

Vincent darted in front of her at a speed she couldn't fathom he possessed. "You can't leave me alone." He grabbed her hand. "Tell me, Maddy, you care for me. Yes?" He walked her to the couch, sat her down. Her answer wasn't important because he continued without hearing one. "So I need you to do me a favor. It'll be fun. Because we're engaged and all." He laughed.

Madelyn's eyes were stuck on his filthy fingers wrapped around her wrist. She was nearly in tears, her voice quivering to keep from crying. "Do we need to make an appearance? Maybe with Mr. Roth or Weinstein." Vincent rocked. "They want to throw an engagement soirée in the roof cabaret. In April. But we can move it. Sooner. That'll be fun." He mumbled to himself. "Right?" He gripped her hand more firmly. "Vincent."

He was on her, holding her face and kissing her. It was violent. It was desperate. She tried to stop him, to scream or curse or yell for help, but he pressed his lips so firmly against hers, she could barely escape to breathe let alone, holler for someone to save her. She attempted to push him away, but he trapped her under all his weight. *Why is he doing this? What's wrong with him? He doesn't even like me. He doesn't even like girls!*

He roared. "I know!" He flung himself to the other side of the couch. "I know." He began to melt into a pool of snot and tears and sweat and spit.

Madelyn scrambled to her feet and grabbed a candlestick from a shelf. "You know what? What do you know?" She should have been running. She should be banging on every door, screaming for someone to tame the madman in her apartment. But she knew Vincent, and this wasn't him. And he...he had *heard* her. Even when she couldn't say anything because he was on top of her, he responded to what she'd been thinking.

He crawled in her direction.

"Don't move." She raised the candlestick above her head. "So help me God, I'll knock you so hard the maid'll be cleaning up salt *and* brains in the morning."

He faced forward, looking at nothing in particular. His gaze was vacant. His speech was labored. "I can hear your thoughts. Anyone's. Since the last test."

"You're scaring me. You've *been* scaring me."

He laughed. "You don't even know scared. You haven't seen the things I've seen. Done the things I've done." He finally acknowledged his bloody hands. He rolled up his sleeve and showed her the additional gore stained into his white shirt. More tears streamed down his face. "Do you know how to gain gifts?"

"This is about that…that club you all are in. I told you I'm not interested."

"Sight gives you Sight. Speech gives you Speech."

"You need to go, Vincent. You need to go and you need to stop doing whatever you're doing with those people."

He locked his eyes on hers. "I can't. We're too far now. I'm close to being Complete. It wants me to finish."

"What does?"

"Teacher." He strained to speak. "The entity."

Madelyn had never been conscious of having a soul. Most people aren't. But in that moment she felt hers shiver. It retreated into the farthest recesses of her body, hidden inside the marrow of the deepest bone. That man was terrifying. "Help!" she yelled, running for the door. "Somebody!" She reached for the doorknob, turned, and pulled. It slammed shut. Again, she tried and again it closed.

"It wants you to stay," he said. He lowered his eyelids as he searched for something to recite. "The Complete Man must master all things. Good, Evil. Light, Dark. Right, Left. Silence, Revelry. Male." He opened his eyes and looked to her.

"Female." He rose. "It's one of the last two things I need to do. And it's the least horrific." He sobbed again. "But probably the most challenging." He walked over to her. "I thought this would work. We're engaged. I know it's all a stunt, but to keep it up, we'll have to keep going. Marriage. Kids." Again, he began to wobble. He cupped his face in his hands. "I thought I'd get it over with. I can't. I can't to you, I can't to him." He cried into his palm. His sobs were anguished and heavy, seeming to come from as low as his heels. "Oh, it hurts to love. It's good to love. Even if I love someone who can't make me Complete." He slid his hands to his lips and he kissed them. He reached for her and laid one on her cheek. She flinched at the touch. "I apologize. You can break off the engagement, and I will make sure you don't lose your job." He turned away and went to the window.

"Where are you going?"

He opened it.

She was afraid to move closer. "What...what're you doing?"

He stuck one leg out. "I'm saving you." He swung his other leg over the side, and he sat on the ledge.

"Vincent..."

"Don't move that salt. At least for a few more days." He gripped the sill, and with a silent *one, two, three*, he threw himself out.

Madelyn shrieked and ran to the open window. She leaned over as far as she could and extended her arm like it was possible for her to catch him from four stories up.

Below, Vincent landed delicately on his feet and ran around the corner, not looking back.

❖

The final dress rehearsal for the Ali Baba number was scheduled to begin in fifteen minutes. In it, the whole cast would tell the story of how a poor man, played by Vincent, outsmarted forty thieves and took their treasure for himself and his humble wife who was, without surprise, portrayed by Madelyn. It was a real rags-to-riches type of story with original songs by Salvatore. There was a lot of buzz around what kind of extravagant sets and costumes would be revealed. That, according to Weinstein, was the most important aspect of the twelve-minute production number. "If you're all terrible, at least the stage will look beautiful," he said before they started. This rehearsal was the cast's last chance to show him they would be just as good as, if not better than, any piece of painted lumber behind them.

"Fifteen 'til places," Eric, the stage manager, hollered over and over again as he walked through the halls. Several chorus members yelled back a *thank you*, but all Madelyn could do was shudder. In just fifteen minutes, she'd have to be onstage with Vincent again. She'd become a nervous wreck trying to face him every day at the show. Sure, she could have walked, but she liked the work. She'd abandoned her old life to move to the city because she wanted to be onstage. And *Weinstein's Wonderacts* was the best show in town with the largest paychecks. Leaving was a silly idea. That night with Vincent was just that. *A* night. At least that was what she convinced herself of. While he hadn't shown any more signs of aggression, he'd become distant. Disconnected. Sometimes manic.

One moment he'd argue with Weinstein about a direction, like he knew more than a man who'd been in the business for thirty years, and the next he'd be sitting in the wings staring at the catwalk like it was his first time in a theater. In their numbers together, he'd barely make eye contact with her. His gaze always landed somewhere below hers, on her cheekbones or nostrils. They were supposed to play lovers, but every time they were to embrace, he kept at least two inches between them. Their charm was tarnished and Madelyn knew everyone noticed, but they were too afraid to say anything for fear of him having an episode. Vincent was, after all, the star, and stars aren't great about receiving notes. Madelyn thought of all this every night before walking onstage. She began to dread the lights she used to love so dearly. And a new number was enough to make her faint. When Weinstein cracked jokes about the cast being awful, she knew he was talking about the chemistry between Ali and his wife.

She sat at her makeup table to apply the last jewel to her brow. A tedious task like that momentarily took her mind off her troubles. It was just her and that darn jewel.

Rita popped her head in the door. She was draped in royal blue, emerald, and gold, an enchanted, wise-cracking peacock that helps Ali discover the secret words to open the door to the cave. She squawked a terribly irritating sound and laughed.

Madelyn dropped the gemstone she'd been trying to put on, and she huffed.

"Oh, I'm sorry. Let me help," Rita said. She entered the dressing room and pulled up a chair. "I've been making bird sounds at everyone, trying to break the tension. Everyone is so nervous." She found the stone and held it up. Madelyn half smiled and nodded in appreciation. "Gee, not you, too. You're always so charming when everyone else is being a beast."

"The number's not good, Rita."

"I guess they'll just have to make my feathered headdress larger to distract everyone." She laughed louder than necessary to try and lighten her spirits.

Madelyn hardly noticed. Her mind wandered back to her

co-star. She had to say something or she'd explode. "You're close with Vincent. You socialize outside the theater?"

"Yes." Rita made a queer face. "Don't worry. We're not having an affair, if that's what you're wondering." She chuckled to herself and placed her hand on Madelyn's shoulder. "I think you and I both know there's no risk."

While Rita continued to find humor in her joke, Madelyn's chest tightened. The secret was working its way out. "He came to me."

Rita stopped mid-guffaw. Her jaw opened larger than a gargoyle's. "Listen, it's none of my business what people do behind closed doors." She cupped her head in her hands. "Christ, I'm sorry. I didn't know you two were really..." She gathered her blue train and stood up. "I always say the wrong thing."

Madelyn pulled her back down, begging her to stay. She gravely stared at her. "He's not well."

Rita leaned her chair back and peeked into the hallway. She nodded and returned the chair to the ground. "I can't really say exactly what—"

A scream pierced through the innards of the theater. "Help!" Eric called from one floor below. "We need help!" They heard him hurl himself down the twisting metal stairs to the stage level. "It's Vincent!"

Madelyn and Rita's eyes met.

In mere seconds, the hallway was congested with cast members pouring from their dressing rooms. The stairwell was so clogged, Madelyn and Rita could only get as far as the doorway. The cries and gasps and screams coming from below were deafening. That tiny corridor echoed all sound up to the roof and back again.

Salvatore's voice stood out among the others. Madelyn heard him grunt as he pushed through the crowd. "What happened? What happened?" His voice was higher and more desperate than anything Madelyn had ever heard, caught between a wail and a shriek.

Then there was silence.

Madelyn shoved through to the railing. She leaned over and saw Sal standing in the doorway to Vincent's dressing room.

At first he just released a quiet "No." Then he yelled, "No!" He tried to enter, but a stagehand pulled him back. "Let me go!" He struggled. "Get off me...Vince!" His knees buckled and he fell. "Vincent..."

Madelyn turned away. Rita caught her in her arms. She didn't know what they saw down there, but she knew it wasn't good. What happened between them that night was a warning, a cry for help. Something terrible was haunting that man. It seemed that something finally got to him.

❖

The car ride was quieter without him. His usual laugh wasn't ringing in her ear. Her left hand was still heavy, though. The ring she'd once resented was now a somber reminder of a friend's generosity. Yes, a friend. A good friend. Even though they never shared a true romance or spent much time together that wasn't staged, Vincent had been kind to her. Almost more than anybody else, he recognized her talent. He chose her to be the one on his arm because, as he said, "You deserve the spotlight, baby." Except for that one time just nights before his death, he'd been a joy to work with. A sob caught in her throat as she thought about how seemingly arbitrary and rapid his decline was.

"I'm sorry we have to put you through this," said Harold. "Mourning should never be this public."

She shrugged and pulled the belt on her black coat tighter. "Our whole relationship was public. I suppose it's only fitting for it to end this way."

"You don't have to say anything to anyone out there."

"I won't."

He was quiet for a moment. "Good. Thank you." He picked at his fingernails to avoid eye contact. "The press has been relentless. They surely don't need more fuel for the fire."

"I didn't think suicides were reported in the papers. Back home it'd be in terribly bad taste."

Harold hummed. "This is New York. We reserve good taste for museums. And he was such a public figure. It'd be difficult to get around it."

"Pills," she sighed. "He must have really been at war with himself."

Harold didn't agree or disagree. He instead looked out the window and said, "It's been a long week."

She sensed there was more to that thought. "Are you troubled by something else, Mr. Roth?"

He took out a handkerchief and blotted his forehead. "I…ah, in addition to all this, a business partner of mine has disappeared. Nothing compared to what we are dealing with presently, but it does occasionally steal my attention." He laughed. It wasn't an expression of humor, but the sound of being at the end of one's rope. "We will need vacations after this, Miss Vicks. We are now far too aware of how delicate the human mind can be. Let us henceforth be more careful with our own and the ones of those we love."

She shook her head, somberly smiled, and closed her eyes. She allowed thoughts of oncoming flashing cameras and nosy journalists to dissolve. Behind them, was the farm, flat, golden, and calm.

Hasis

Winter 1923

Once upon a time, he was darker, with olive complexion and coal-black hair, but years avoiding the sun had made his skin delicate, almost translucent, or in some light, opalescent. He didn't have an allergy or physical aversion to sunshine; he simply chose not to flaunt his odd form in front of the normal folk. He was tired of stares. One would think after all this time, he'd be accustomed to awkward looks, but he wasn't. And he couldn't blame people for the attention. He was so tall, he had to bend his knees when going through most doorways. His spindly shape was covered in cloaks of linen or wool, depending on the season. The few who laid eyes on him would be confused whether he was a monk, a sorcerer, or a derelict. Hasis was the kind of man who would frighten a child. Even if it wasn't with malevolent intention, his glance often sent people into hysteria or chilled the spines of men three times his weight. As a result, he had few interactions with others.

One can't sequester oneself for so long without consequence. For Hasis, social graces began to wane, daydreams became real, and ideas darkened. He came to the New World in its infancy. Like the others on those wooden ships, he had a dream. That continent would refresh him, bring him out of the shadows. The Eastern earth hadn't been polluted with Christendom, so he could form his own way of life based on truer beliefs. He could found a new city that embraced them, just like the settlements of the Old Days. Those were glorious times. And while he was moderately successful for some while, he underestimated the very forces that drove him into seclusion to begin with. They, too, came over on wooden boats and they infiltrated the minds of settlers. Again, the Way of Things was eradicated. Hasis was pushed back into obscurity. Social graces diminished, daydreams became delusions, and ideas became violent.

"Good morning, friend," he said.

A bird whistled from the treetops.

"Come down and greet me." He held out his finger. A small finch plunged from overhead and landed on him. It was a common brown bird, but with a rose-colored face and breast, like it had been dipped in a jar of jam. He admired its blush. "Look at you. Painted for war, you are."

The finch chirped again.

Hasis closed his eyes and focused on the bird's little brain. He struggled to recall a very old, forgotten language. Once it came to him, he thought, *Does the sage still grow in the Astor garden?*

The bird gave him an affirmative signal.

Bring it. Hasis raised his hand and let the finch fly in the direction of the decrepit mansion.

He'd been able to gather the other ingredients—spices and minerals from faraway places—but something as common as sage had been oddly hard to acquire. He couldn't bear the thought of going into town for it, so the bird would do. In recent years, he'd stopped asking other beings for help. Like the humans, animals were becoming just as far removed from the Way. Few could understand the languages of old that once linked all life on earth. But every so often, one would cross his path and surprise him. That purple finch was becoming a true companion.

For that reason, he made sure to hide the chicken feet from its view when it returned with several leaves in its beak. Even though chickens and finches are vastly different birds, they are birds nonetheless. Distant cousins. It could have been discouraging for the poor thing to see those stiff, curled talons detached from their feathered body.

Hasis went through the curtains into his cave to prepare the spell. The layers of fabric and rugs barely kept out the cold morning air. He whispered a chant and snapped his fingers to ignite the wicks of a dozen candles. Their fire seemed to cut the chill. He emptied a jar of white sand into a silver bowl, added the sage, and crushed it together with a pestle. He rocked in a hypnotic rhythm as he blended, his nostrils flaring to capture the aroma of exotic soil and herb. Sage grew wild in the East. He recalled his youth there as he extracted its oils and blended them with the sea salts. Even the silver bowl had a scent to him, tangy and adolescent. It was the metal his family wore. The fragrance was so specific to his childhood, it almost hurt to remember.

Running down the coast with the others.

Banquets of meats in rich broths and fruits from faraway lands.

The bracelet he outgrew, the one with the green stones.

His mother's laugh. Her cries.

A more contemporary odor sliced through his memories, reminding him of his current, sad existence. He knew that smell. Talc and something else. He sniffed the air. Beeswax.

The combination was familiar. Only one other person had smelled of such things, and that person was dead. Another perfume invaded his airspace, one of flowers that were not scheduled to bloom for several months. That too was traceable to a very specific human, one he'd only recently met. Hasis barreled through the cave opening.

"There he is," said Rita. She stood less than twenty paces away, pointing her finger directly at him. A young man raced past her. He was slender with long legs that devoured the short distance between them in a matter of seconds. His black hair glistened in the morning sun, just like Vincent's used to when he visited.

"You monster!" screamed the man. He was getting closer and closer.

"Sal, no!" begged Rita as she ran after him.

As soon as the man stepped onto the smooth stone in front of him, Hasis raised his hand and looked him in the eye. The man fell to the ground. "I assume this is the lover," Hasis said. "Salvatore, is it?"

Rita helped Sal up. He groaned as he struggled to stand.

Hasis glared at him, forcing his body back to the ground. "I recognize the grease in his hair. Vincent wore the same."

Sal's face was pressed against rock. He struggled to speak. "You killed him."

Hasis paid him no mind. "Why have you brought him, witch?"

Rita huffed, swiped hair from her forehead. "Because Vincent is dead."

Hasis sighed. "An unfortunate turn of events. He was so close to his goal."

Rita stood to confront him. She was shockingly short in comparison. "Something terrible, something *evil* came through. You had to have known what he was getting himself into and still you—"

"Silence!" roared Hasis. His stare struck her straight through the center of her pupils, shrinking them to the size of a pencil point. Her mouth snapped shut. "That is better." He panted. "You do not want to be at odds with me, witch. I am far older and far more *influential* than you can ever imagine." He articulated every word with intensity and precision. "Vincent was on his way to becoming a powerful wizard. You saw this, yes?" He waited for a response, forgetting he'd shut her up just seconds before. He snapped his fingers to unclamp her jaw.

"Yes." She massaged her cheek with her hand. "He was close."

"Then I believe that makes the guidance I provided useful. There is no reason to come to my home with such force." Hasis was suddenly exasperated. He leaned over to calm himself and catch his breath. Through deep wheezes, he continued. "This entity you summoned is aggressive, but not responsible for what happened to him." A sudden bolt of pain shot through his head. He grunted and stumbled to his knee. His left eye stung. He wiped it with his index finger. When he pulled it away, blood dribbled down his hand.

Salvatore was released from his invisible grasp. "You're sick, aren't you?" he asked. He reached for Rita for help to his feet.

Ruddy tears streamed down Hasis's face. "No, no. Just out of practice. I haven't been forced to use these muscles in a long, long time. They thank you for the exercise." He chuckled, pulled his bench forward, and sat. His heart beat with more force and speed than it had in many years. He felt nervous. Maybe the boy was right. Perhaps he was ill. But that couldn't be. He was Immortal, and Immortals are not susceptible to what ails humans. He concentrated on his breathing to relax. He inhaled the remnants of sage on his fingertips. That brought him peace.

"Then what happened?" Sal asked.

Hasis watched Salvatore's veins plump as he balled his hands into little fists. He could almost hear adrenaline rush through his system, zipping through him with the sound of a hissing snake. After such a loss, most people would be left with what they described as actual holes in their souls. Emptiness radiated from them in what Hasis saw as a gray-blue haze. But not from the man before him. Salvatore was indeed plagued by grief, but it was accompanied by a red-hot kernel of anger. With every passing second, it grew. He was a volcano ready to ruin everything in its path. "My, my. You are *full* of fury."

Sal bit his lip, rolled his shoulders. "Do you know what it's like to lose the only person you've ever loved?"

Hasis felt his heart sear. Tears stung the back of his eyes, but he wouldn't allow them to reach air. "Young man, you have no idea what I know, what I have suffered."

Rita placed her hand on Sal's arm to calm him. "Just tell us what you know."

"You tell me. How did he die?" asked Hasis. He watched them silently try to decide who would be the one to tell the tale. "Come now. I do not have the periodicals delivered to this place." He smiled.

"That wouldn't do any good anyway. The papers say it was a suicide."

With a quivering jaw, Sal spoke. "We found him in his dressing room. Lying down. Every bone in his body crushed. No blood. No bruising. No poison. No signs of struggle." He breathed deeply to compose himself, but it only triggered sadness. "And definitely no pills." He fell to his knees and wept.

Hasis averted his eyes. He was struggling with his own feelings, and he had no need to see those of that human. He spoke above Salvatore's wails. "Vincent was a prideful man. Tortured, yes, but certainly not enough to take his own life."

Sal snapped. "We know that."

"So the entity must have done it," said Rita. "Vincent had been frightened of it for weeks."

Hasis groaned and rose to his feet. "The *entity* is not made of flesh and bone like you and I. It is from a spirit realm. I do not see how it could have manifested physically to inflict such harm."

"Well, a *person* certainly didn't do this," Rita said. "It's impossible."

"Oh, but you are wrong. This seems like magic, a destructive kind that only mortals can practice." He narrowed his gaze at her.

She gasped. "Are you suggesting I had something to do with it?"

"If not you, surely someone you know."

"What about you?" asked Sal. He stood to meet him. "Maybe you did it. You know magic."

Hasis was amused. His high, mocking laugh cut through the air, echoing from the other caves on the cliff side. "But I am not mortal."

Rita and Sal's confusion was apparent. They looked to each other, not sure how to proceed. "I don't understand," she finally said.

"When I take you down or shut you up or…" He thought, smiled. "When I do this." He nodded at Salvatore.

Sal's knees wobbled. His right leg stepped forward,

followed by his left. Then his left leg returned. Then his right. He kept repeating these steps, over and over.

Hasis clapped on the beat. "What a marvelous dancer you are, young man!"

Sal shrieked. "I can't stop!"

Hasis nodded once more.

Sal's legs abruptly stopped. He stumbled.

Hasis's grin was maniacal. "That, my dear, is *power, not magic*. And I was born with it." He noticed his small fire had died. He'd need a larger one to prepare his lunch. He reached for a fresh piece of wood from the corner. "I have told you before, all of my kind possesses advanced capabilities. The *magic* your kind learns simply attempts to replicate what comes naturally to me. It is primitive and imperfect. If I wanted to kill Vincent, I'd have done it in a much more impressive way." He turned to Salvatore. "Vincent was instructing your Circle. He taught you his tricks. Surely you know an incantation to create a simple flame."

"I do." Sal cleared his throat. "I know of one."

"Please." Hasis extended his hand in the direction of the fire.

Salvatore closed his eyes and whispered a chant. He followed it with a hand gesture. The tip of the branch caught fire.

Hasis raised his eyebrows, pleased. "See? You are capable of magic." He put his hands on Salvatore's shoulders and guided him down to the same level as the flame. "Fire. It gives us heat and light, but it kills this wood and produces suffocating smoke. Productive magic. Destructive magic. Positive and negative. Two poles. All magic is like this. And all your friends with knowledge of it are capable of embracing either side." Hasis closed his eyes and spoke directly into Sal's mind. *Who in your Circle could be responsible?*

❖

After the chicken feet had charred, he ground them down to dust, then blended it into a paste using a combination of bodily fluids from several animals and men. He spat into the bowl, set it aside. The smell was repulsive, even to a recluse like Hasis.

He retrieved the silver bowl containing the sand, sage, and various memories. Before he ruined it with that putrid black muck, he inhaled one last time. The grip he felt around his head seemed to loosen. His heart slowed to a more acceptable rhythm. His eyes were lubricated with clean tears, not blood. A youthful smile painted itself between newly formed dimples.

This place and the lifestyle it forced him into was destroying him. He had to go home. It was a terrible idea to stay in New York as long as he had. The East still had true followers of the Way. Tribes and families had disbanded, but they could still be tracked down. As soon as he finished his work on that wretched island, he'd leave.

With a sigh, he spilled the sand onto the Magic Squares, which he'd arranged in the same position he'd instructed Vincent to use in his ritual. He smoothed it flat with a brush made of white hair and used a wooden spoon to dig a hole in the center. He dumped the paste into it, lit incense at sacred points, and began his spell.

It was time to secure the openings Vincent had made in the veil between worlds.

SALVATORE

Spring 1923

Their last day together was a scratch in the record of Salvatore's life. It played over and over and over and over.

"What is this?" Vincent asked. He held a sheet of yellowing paper in his hands.

Sal dove for it, snatched it from his grasp. "None of your business," he said. "This is a private matter."

Vincent let out a thunderous laugh. "Private? We have no secrets between us. Let me see." He tried to grab it back.

Sal ran away, jumped onto the bed, and held the paper high above his head. "It's nothing."

"People don't make such efforts to hide *nothing*." He looked at Vincent mournfully. "Let me see."

Sal bit his lip and huffed in frustration. "It's just a song. A personal one. Not for the show."

A genuine grin appeared on Vincent's face. "Are you writing love songs about someone?"

Sal blushed. "Stop."

"You are, you devil. Who could it be about?" He joyfully skipped to the bed like an excited ballerina.

"Very funny."

Vince's face got serious. "This better not be about Madelyn Vicks." He lowered his voice. "She's a taken lady."

Sal's expression darkened. "I don't like jokes like that and you know it."

"Oh, don't be such a sour apple," Vince said. A very purposefully large smile spread across his face. "I'm just being smart."

Sal let his legs give out so he could drop onto the now-messy sheets. "It's not fair. She hardly knows you. At least pick a friend, like Clarissa, to masquerade with." He looked at the many scribbles on that sheet of paper. Lyrics had been written, crossed out, and rewritten one hundred times. Even in song, Sal didn't have a grasp on his feelings for Vincent.

"You know that wouldn't work." Vincent crawled to his side and put his chin on his shoulder. "No matter what the dailies say, I love you. Not Madelyn."

Sal exhaled something that was half laugh, half cry.

Vince's eyes widened with encouragement. "And what do you say to somebody who tells you they love you?"

Sal scooted to the edge of the mattress. "I know." He stood and looked at him. "I know you love me." He walked to the piano.

"Well," Vincent said, settling his back on the headboard. "I was expecting to hear something sweeter in response."

He stacked the papers neatly in their proper place and met Vince's eyes. "You know how I feel about you."

It was Vincent's turn to avert his gaze. "Yes. But sometimes it's just nice to hear it said."

Again, Salvatore looked at the pages of mutilated poetry. He knew he had lovely things to say, but he didn't quite know how to do it. There were feelings there, feelings he tried very hard to suppress or brush away. To acknowledge them would be acknowledging the difficulties they faced. He didn't know if he was ready to do that. Life was already tricky enough. "We should get to rehearsal soon. It's a big day."

❖

Mr. Weinstein was doing his best to brighten the cast's spirits. This was a perilous task, as his usual trick of throwing a party wasn't appropriate. Nobody wanted to dress in extravagant outfits and cut a rug on the dance floor after the death of the show's star. They were grieving. No matter what anybody thought of Vincent, nobody could deny his magnetism, both on and off the stage. With him dead, the life force of the production also seemed to have expired. Gone were the days of him wandering the halls, singing and reciting something ridiculous to raise their energy before show time. And his numbers were gone from the program. They tested an understudy for three days, but audiences didn't take to him. Vincent's songs were *Vincent's* and nobody else's. They held many meetings about how to proceed and decided that when it was time to introduce a new star, he'd get completely original material so no one could draw comparisons. Until that could happen, the cast performed the show with holes where Vincent used to be. *Weinstein's Wonderacts* was beginning to feel like a sinking ship without its captain at the helm. The cast sensed they were in danger of arriving at the stage door one day to find it locked, a closing notice nailed over the sign.

So Weinstein used his connections and his money to ease everyone's minds with performances of classical piano and Spanish guitar played between shows. Dinners were held in the lounge and flowers delivered to dressing rooms—anything to erase the ghostly expressions from the faces of his cast. Private screenings of films in the rooftop garden pavilion were particularly successful. It was still winter, so its giant glass panels were closed and the terrace was covered with a heavy tent.

He squealed as he walked in front of the screen before the lights went down. "This film," he said, "was sent to me from an old collaborator in Germany." Several people in the room groaned. He paid them no mind. "We are the first Americans to see it. It should be a real treat."

"What is it?" asked Salvatore. He sat in the back row, his shoulders hunched over crossed legs and arms. "Another film for the rabble? Want to make us laugh again?"

Rita nudged him and widened her eyes.

"What?" He blew out a stream of smoke. "They're silly." Typically they were shown comedies starring Keaton, Arbuckle, or Chaplin. Salvatore, at least in recent weeks, had become darker and found the likes of those men intolerable. The music and the dinners and the flowers he could stomach, even appreciate, but those awful comedies made him feel ill, made him feel manipulated into happiness. His lips were frozen in a long straight line, and he was uninterested in discovering whether or not the corners of his mouth could even turn up into a smile anymore.

"Actually," Weinstein said, "it's something more *frightening*." The room buzzed. "I thought it'd be a nice change of pace."

Sal inhaled on his cigarette and raised his eyebrows, intrigued.

Weinstein looked at a card in his hand. "It's called *Nosferatu*." Several dancers laughed at the name. "It's the story of Dracula."

A handful of people got up and left. The idea of a film like that was too much to handle. They didn't need more darkness in their lives. It was hard for the cast to fathom how someone they'd been so close to could have hidden such despair. They felt vulnerable and stupid. But those in the Circle felt worse. They were aware of his dabbling in dangerous magic. Hell, they even encouraged it. Those people silently mourned and kept to themselves. Some even swore off ever practicing magic again.

Even though he was the closest to the atrocity, Sal remained seated. His interest was piqued. He'd read *Dracula* years ago and quite liked it. He recalled feeling sadness for the Count, despite his monstrous persona. Why was that? He peered into the recesses of his mind for an answer but couldn't find one.

Before any thorough investigation could be done, the lights dimmed, and the projector clicked to life.

❖

As soon as he returned home from the screening, Salvatore tore apart his room for his copy of *Dracula*. Once he found it, he devoured the novel, finishing it in a single night. The only time he paused was to note one of Bram Stoker's more poignant lines, something the Count had said to Jonathan Harker about finding contentment in seclusion and shadow: "And my heart, through weary years of mourning over the dead, is not attuned to mirth." He read it over and over again, finally marking the line with a heavy, black circle. *That*, he thought, *is the truth.*

Like the monster on the screen and in the book, bereavement had hardened Sal's heart. Did Dracula also fail to tell the ones he mourned for of his love for them? Surely Vincent knew. It was obvious, wasn't it? He had to stop thinking about it.

He went to work because he had to, played the piano during performances and at rehearsals without much passion or effort. He was an excellent musician, so vacantly getting through a handful of songs was easy. He tried socializing, but he found it difficult to ignite any real desire to be around others. Conversations were dull with everyone but Vince. And he was suspicious of almost every person at the Duchess. If Dark Magic was being used against Vincent by another member of the Circle, that magician was most likely within arm's length, breathing the same air and secretly laughing at what they'd gotten away with.

It was almost too much to even fathom. He pushed the thought away.

He'd rather just stay home in bed. Let his mind go blank. There were mornings when he'd wake up with the sun because he was tired of sleeping, of dreaming of Vincent, but being awake was just as wearisome. He often just lay there and stared at the ceiling, caught in limbo between slumber and consciousness. He'd rest there for hours and hours with absolutely no motivation to rise. Several times he panicked at the thought of being stuck there, that his brain would never move his limbs and make him stand. It would take him actually speaking aloud—"Get up, Sal!"—for his mournful trance to disappear.

Or he'd be woken by a visitor, like Rita.

"Sal, open up," she said from the other side of the door. "You can't just seclude yourself for the rest of eternity."

He groaned. Nothing intelligible, just a sound of annoyance made loud enough for her to hear.

"Oh, you're some kind of ogre now?" She paused to hear a laugh. He didn't give her one. "Okay, I'm coming in." The lock clicked. She opened the door.

Salvatore sprung to life. "How'd you do that?"

She threw her purse down. "I'm capable of learning a simple spell like turning a goddamned lock." She wrestled with an oversized scarf. Once it was off, she threw it over a chair and panted. "Vince taught me. The ol' charm and gesture." She took off her coat. "Gee, it's cold out there. Almost April and it's still this frigid."

"Greenland is melting," Sal said. He searched for his shirt somewhere among the twisted sheets.

"Excuse me?"

"I read it in the paper. One scientist believes there are secrets hidden under the ice."

She chuckled. "Was this scientist named Jules Verne, by chance?"

"What if it's true? What if we find Atlantis or a dinosaur kingdom?" He thought for a moment, stared at the skyline in front of him. "Or a Hellmouth. Maybe the heat from there is melting it."

"I don't think that's very likely." Rita folded her coat neatly and observed the clothes scattered all over the floor. She shook her head.

For the first time since she arrived, he looked at her. "Why isn't it likely? You and Vincent did it here. Who is to say it couldn't be done there? Maybe it was even the same spell."

She was visibly irked by that. "Sal, we didn't open a portal to hell." He averted his eyes. She made a point to move into his line of vision. "You know that, right?"

"I don't know what I know anymore." He wasn't sure why he was bringing this up. Or maybe he wanted to pick a fight with her. He needed to feel something, even if it was anger.

Rita tried not let him bait her, but she turned as red as a tomato. "It was another witch that killed him."

"But what you brought through wasn't good either. You have to know that. It made him scared and anxious and caused him pain and gave him nosebleeds and—"

"I know!" she yelled, stomping her foot against the floor.

The giant window next to her let out a short, loud squeak. Sal turned his attention there.

Rita didn't seem to notice. She dove into a fit. "I don't know why I did it," she said, pacing. "The whole idea sounded crazy. I didn't even fully understand what was being asked of me."

In the spot where he stared, a splinter the size of a staple appeared on the glass.

"But they said it was for the best. And he had so much confidence."

He liked feeling her energy. It was manic. Destructive. The tiny crack grew.

"I thought I'd be able to use this gift for good. I never ever believed it was possible."

He squinted, and the fissure tiptoed across the pane in a sharp, jagged line.

"You have no idea the things I see. It's terrible," she said.

The pane began to fracture in opposite directions.

"Can you imagine growing up afraid of something deep within you that you have no control over?"

Oh, he could more that imagine that. He'd felt it. His whole life. Probably just as much as she had, maybe even more. The glass spiderwebbed into a thousand tiny fissures.

"And then after all that time, being told that you're fine. That you're special?"

That brought him out of his trance. He whipped his head in her direction. "No," he said. He spoke like his words were poison, and he needed to spit them out. "I can't imagine that. Nobody has ever told me I'm fine. Only Vincent. And now he's dead." He burned his eyes into hers as he waited for that to sink in.

Every muscle in her face fell. "Sal, I'm so sorry this happened."

He pointed to the window. "Look what we've done."

She turned and clutched her heart. "We?"

"You started it. I finished. Or maybe it was the other way around. Who knows? No words necessary. Our emotions are very powerful."

"I think we all need to stop practicing magic. It's dangerous."

"No." He lay back down and twirled his hair around his index finger. "I know what's dangerous. Complacency."

Rita sat down on the corner of the bed. "We're scared, Sal. We don't know who it was that killed him. What if it was a friend or colleague or someone we sleep next to at night?"

He stared suspiciously at her. "Yes. I hear you're quite popular in that department." She blushed. "Maybe you're all in cahoots. Get rid of the star so you can take his place."

She tried to touch him. "You know that's not true."

He turned away. "I want to be alone."

"Please. Let me help you. I'll buy you lunch."

"Get out."

She sat on the bed, still and teary-eyed.

He lunged forward. "I said, get out!" He howled a foreign phrase and raised his hand. Thousands of shards of glass lifted from the window and raced toward Rita. She screamed, and the glass stopped and spun in the air. The sharp pieces tinkled menacingly near Rita's back. She cowered. "Now," he said.

Without speaking, she ducked for her coat and ran out the door. As it slammed, the glass fell and blanketed everything in the room.

The elements were free to penetrate the apartment. A gust of wickedly cold wind picked up a song he'd tried to write but never finished and liberated his half-formed lyrics. As he watched them fly above the skyline, Sal could swear he heard them sing back to him. The melody he'd attempted to write for months came to him as naturally as breathing or swallowing or blinking.

If only he still had Vincent around to finally hear that love song.

❖

Sunlight strained to reach the forest floor. Even though branches were bare, providing little obstruction, the path was dim. But that was nothing new. Everything seemed darker to Sal nowadays. Hasis and he could have been walking in summer's brightest light, and he wouldn't have noticed. He'd been drained of his ability to feel any of life's delights, a spectral version of his former self.

"You look unwell," Hasis said. He carried a basket filled with odds and ends he'd found on that morning's stroll.

Sal stared ahead. "You don't look too great yourself," he replied.

Hasis smiled. "You have not been sleeping? Eating?"

"My window's broken. It gets cold at night." Sal crossed his arms and tucked his hands under his armpits for warmth. "There it is." He nodded to a tree in the distance with a tattered purple scarf tied around its trunk.

"A keen eye you have." Hasis picked up his pace and let his long legs propel him quickly to the spot.

Sal wasn't about to exert himself. He'd saunter over when his feet felt like it. He hollered after him, "What exactly are we searching for?"

"It is called Solomon's Seal." Hasis bent down, brushing dead leaves from the ground.

"Spooky."

"The plant is easily recognizable in the spring. Beautiful

white blooms that dangle like jewelry from the stem." He drove his pale fingers into the dirt and scooped it toward the trunk of the tree. "In the winter it is simply a root. A valuable one."

Sal came to his side, squatted to observe. "Can I help you dig?"

"No," Hasis said with a little too much force. He wore an awfully horrified expression, too. He quickly softened it. "I appreciate the offer, but your hands will taint its properties."

"Fine." Salvatore's tolerance for that man—no, that *thing*—was thinning. He'd come to Hasis almost two hours ago and was still waiting for counsel. "Will this take long?"

Hasis stopped excavating and raised his head to look at Sal. "Are you in a rush?"

He suddenly felt small. It was unkind to be so impatient with someone who could potentially offer him assistance. He tried speaking in a kinder tone. "Is this root for my purposes? I'm curious as to what we're doing out here."

Hasis went back to his project. "No. This is for me. But the time we are spending together, that is for you." He tugged on something in the soil and grinned. "Found it." He broke up more earth with his sharp fingernail, then gave the clump a quick blow to clear it away, revealing a long, knotted root. "I have been attempting to discern how charged you are."

"I'm sorry?"

"Emotionally. You are deeply sad. Intensely angry." With a slight yank, he freed the root from the ground and securely wrapped it in his hand. "Such feelings provide fertile ground for magical forces, even for the most mortal of men." He stood, brushed the root clean on his robe. "Vincent felt strongly about many, many things. That is what made him such a successful wizard. That is what brought him so close to becoming Complete."

A perfect mixture of sorrow and pride bubbled within Sal, causing an inadvertent smile. "He would be happy to hear you call him that: a wizard."

"And he would be pleased to see such dedication from you. Look." Hasis cleaned off one of the root's many nubs. "These are the scars left from stems of previous years. If you look closely, it appears to have been stamped with a seal. Legend says King Solomon himself placed his ring upon the plant when he recognized its worth."

"Solomon used that ring to help him command demons without being in danger."

"True."

"So this plant grants protection?"

"Or assists in the summoning of spirits. Or warding them off. Also, to finish certain spells. Very diverse. When used correctly, it can be a very powerful ingredient. That's why the king blessed it."

Sal was sensing a transition in conversation, but Hasis had thus far proved unable to successfully progress matters. He took it upon himself to move forward. "You're sure this won't help summon Vincent's spirit back to me?"

Hasis laughed heartily. "No, my boy. That kind of magic is more advanced than potion making."

Sal fell toward him, grabbed his robes. "Teach me." He was desperate and tired and more miserable than he thought a person could possibly be. "I need him back. I know it can be done."

"Do you? How do you know? Have you seen it on one of your stages? Read about it in a book?"

"I'm serious."

"So am I, young man. Bringing someone back from the dead requires intense dedication. Severe cost. It is not for the weak."

"I have nothing left, don't you understand? People like me, we rarely find companionship."

"No need to speak in riddles, man. There is nobody here to persecute you."

"I loved him!" He crumbled into a heaving mess of limbs at Hasis's feet. "It is so rare to find such love. Without it I am hollow. I can't continue living with this emptiness."

Salvatore was too busy weeping into the ground to see, but Hasis's large eyes had dampened. He stretched his jaw and rolled his head on his neck to shake the emotion back to a deep part of his heart. He kicked Sal away. "Up, up!" he roared. "This behavior is not useful. Cultivate these feelings and refine them to their purest form. That is magic. That will give you the tools to bring him back."

❖

His metronome legs swung in a 4/4 time signature, the same one as the music he'd rehearsed that morning. As he walked through Midtown and listened to his footsteps, he couldn't help relive the experience. Step, step, step, step translated to "Once I loved you…" The next four beats of his feet meeting slick pavement matched the next line, "Oh, how that's changed…"

How common.

Common lyrics, common themes, common melody, common tempo. He recalled a moment while practicing when it all clicked, when he decided he could do it. *I hate this music. I hate these people.* Then he continued plunking out notes, but with more vigor. More violence.

He stalked across Sixth Avenue with equal strength. The heels of his shoes clicked the ground with such force, he thought he might leave a wake of potholes for unsuspecting chorus girls to fall into on the way to their calls. If they stumbled and broke their necks, they'd be spared the inferno waiting for them at curtain. He felt some relief in that.

Then he adjusted the parcel under his coat. Didn't want gunpowder on his new vest.

If he was going to blow up the theater, why did he even bother spending the first several hours of his day going over music with sixteen screeching beauty queens? Because, even though his mental state had withered, Salvatore was trying to get back into a routine—appear more healthy—and playing piano for those hungover canaries every morning at ten o'clock was part of it. After that, he took lunch at noon, read between two and three, napped until five, ate at five thirty, then exercised at six before he had to be back at the theater for a performance. This long stroll down Forty-Third Street would have to count as the latter, even though he didn't consider walking proper exercise. He'd always been too thin, so he was more interested in weight training. A strict set of push-ups and squats was necessary to acquire the physique he desired—the one seen in photographs on the walls of that speakeasy on Thirty-Seventh and Seventh. *That* body was the opposite of the lithe one he possessed, the one he wanted to get in top shape for Vincent. Trekking clear across town wouldn't do much for bulking up, but it would relieve his fears of developing a stomach like all the men on his father's side. And the cool air would clear his head.

You don't need to do this, Sal, said a voice inside his mind.

He shook it away, stepped into a doorway, and lit the last of his cigarettes. He was careful not to bring the lighter too close to the explosives hidden under his coat. After all, this wasn't a suicide mission. He was doing this to teach them a lesson.

RITA

Spring 1923

She didn't feel safe until the door was closed behind her. She turned the lock and set the chain, then leaned her forehead against the frame, still holding the knob. A hot spear of panic pierced her in the back. *This isn't good enough.*

She threw down her bag, wrestled out of her scarf, and stomped over to the sewing table in the corner. Even though Carrie had taught her to stitch, Rita never used the machine. Instead it became a catch-all for everything that didn't have a proper place in the apartment. For almost a year since Carrie died, it'd been collecting trinkets, bills, and baubles. It was all junk, so she slid her arms across the surface to clear it away. The rubbish hit the ground with a crash. She used all her strength to pull the table across the room and barricade the door. If someone was going to use a charm to turn the locks, they'd have to use some old-fashioned brute strength to move that table out of the way shortly after.

She threw off her wool coat and sat on the chair in front of the vanity. She looked in the mirror and gasped at her state. Her face was streaked with what looked like tire marks from crying on her way home from Sal's. She ran her fingers through her hair and exhaled. She squeaked in pain.

A tiny flake of glass was lodged in her middle finger. She pulled it out, releasing a faint stream of blood.

If I hadn't left when I did, would I be covered in these shards?

She'd conquered her fear of ghosts years ago, and other fears like heights and critters and darkness were of no consequence to her. She didn't even dread Death anymore, for she was aware of the existence of a soul. She didn't understand it much, but she knew it was there. The only thing that could frighten her was the one thing she was born to be comfortable with: magic. She'd seen it summon spirits, drive men mad, and kill. The Circle had been formed to gain enlightenment, to help members achieve their dreams. On the surface, those were positive goals. But closer examination revealed them to be selfish and negative. Did anyone practice enchantments that could help others? Hasis spoke of magic's opposing light and dark poles. Why did it always seem to slide to the more sinister of the two?

Her reflection gazed sadly back at her. A certain gloom had always been behind those giant eyes, but she'd been diligent about masking it with humor, with song. At just eighteen years old, she couldn't find the strength to do that anymore. The person in that mirror wasn't Rita; it was Margarite, the girl who didn't trust her gifts, who had no confidence about gaining friends and experiencing romance. She needed to reapply Rita, the woman who wowed audiences, mastered her Paramount, had heaps of support, and wasn't afraid of her heart's complicated feelings. But was she really that person anymore?

Yes. She had to be, so she reached for the jar of cold cream and a rag to clean up her face. When she was finished, she threw the cloth on the table and fumbled for her paintbrush. She dipped it in her homemade pigment—the perfect combination of black and green to make her irises stand out—and made wide strokes under her lower lid.

She saw the corner of the room where the sewing table had been reflected in the left side of the mirror, noticing a smudge there. She licked her thumb and rubbed the spot to remove it, but it wouldn't come clean. The blur on the glass moved like smoke from an extinguished candle.

Her hands shaking, she dropped the brush. She scooted her chair from the vanity as if its surface had been on fire. *Not this. I didn't summon anything.* "Go away!" she yelled. Then she grabbed the mirror, tore it from the wall, and threw it to the ground. "You're not getting in here." She scurried through the apartment, plundering everything with a reflective surface. Vases and candlesticks and jars, even polished silver spoons could not escape the purge. She threw it all in a great pile and covered it with a quilt. "I don't give you permission to be here. Go back to that other realm."

Rita paced across the apartment trying to recall a helpful spell or incantation that Vincent had taught the Circle. She pulled at her hair. "Ouch!" Another piece of glass. Damn him. Vincent hadn't bestowed any valuable information on them, just silly incantations to make inanimate objects fly around the room. She could start a fire, she could turn a doorknob, but she couldn't do anything useful like protect herself from a malicious spirit. "Wait!" she said aloud.

Salt.

She darted for the kitchen table, grabbed the salt shaker, and began spinning in circles. She waved her hand manically in the air, dusting white crystals all over the floor and her body.

What else...what else...what else...?

"Your name!" She was grinning and laughing and almost

crying. "I can control you with your name." But what was the entity's name? *That's right.* "Teacher!" She waited for a sign. The room was quiet. "You said that's what we should call you. That's your name. Now go away."

Deep down she knew that wasn't enough. To control an entity like that, she had to use its true name given at Creation. A wave of fear washed over her as she realized this. It seemed to drain her life force, shriveling her up like jerky. If she hadn't hidden all the mirrors, she imagined her reflection would show her skin as gray as a corpse.

A cool sensation danced across the back of her neck. It moved down her body and settled at her ankles. She could feel it even through her heavy black hose. She wanted to flee. "Move, Rita," she said. But it was no use. She was frozen in place with fright. Her brain refused to connect with her feet. She recalled the haphazard circle of salt she stood in. She closed her eyes and repeated, "I'm safe here. I'm safe here," over and over again.

The chilly feeling returned, but this time it manifested as a breeze that caused the white granules near her heels to move. The salt rolled across the floor into two neat piles. The wind elongated them into lines. The center of each line dented, creating two distinct letters: *CC*

Blood raced from her heart and filled every vein with excitement, with relief. "Carrie," she said. "Carrie Connor."

❖

Elisabeth stepped into the hall and embraced Rita. "My girl," she said.

Rita stood rigidly in her arms, not sure how to react to such warmth from a stranger.

Elisabeth released her, backed up, and smiled. "You have

grown." Then she came back in and cupped her hands around Rita's face. "I never thought I'd see you again."

Rita was becoming more and more uncomfortable with this intimacy. "I can't say I remember much about you," she said. "But when I found this"—she held up the old edition of the *New York Herald*—"I felt compelled to find you."

Elisabeth peered down the hall. "Come inside, please." She pulled Rita in, closed the door behind her, and secured several locks. She took the paper from her hands and thumbed through it. "You were quite taken with this when you visited." She flipped it over and opened it to the comics page. The paper was torn right below the *Little Nemo in Slumberland* cartoon. "I suppose this is why it has taken so long."

Rita plunged her hand into her coat pocket and produced a yellowed piece of paper, the missing part of the page. "But my aunt kept it. I guess she thought it might come in handy after all." She nodded at the couch. "May I?"

"By all means. Tea?"

She shook her head. "I'm fine, thank you." She sat on the corner of the sofa, hardly relaxed. "She came to me today. Showed me where she hid your address. In a tin of pins near the sewing machine. She knew I'd never look in there." She gazed out the corner of her eye and laughed. "I find sewing tedious."

Elisabeth settled into her rigid chair. "All these years I thought of you. I worried. So many girls get lost in their gifts. They go mad. I contemplated visiting hospitals to find you."

Rita held up her hand. "I'm well. Thank you." She thought for a moment, wrinkled her brow. "But I'm still unsure how this all works. When Carrie came to me today, she wasn't like the others. I couldn't see her."

"Because she passed on." Elisabeth cleared her throat. "She moved to the other side. I helped her. That is what I do.

That is what women with our Paramount are *meant* to do."
She nervously patted the hair around her ears with her spindly
fingers, ensuring it was tightly secured in its bun. "I had
intentions to train you, but your aunt would have none of it.
Even when she came to me after death, I begged her to show
me to you. She refused. She was very fearful and wanted you
to live a normal life."

Rita chuckled, wiped her eyes. "I'm afraid that's
impossible now."

"She must have had a change of heart." Elisabeth reached
for her hand. "Once a spirit has passed on, it is difficult for
them to return to this plane. So she most likely sent you signs,
yes?"

Rita nodded.

"Your aunt is still watching you. Even though you cannot
speak to her like you can with others, she is here."

Rita felt as if she could rocket to the moon with happiness.
"She wanted me to come here to meet you, to learn from you."

"I believe so. Never has it been more important for
followers of the Way of Things to band together."

Rita cocked her head. "I've heard that before."

"What?"

"The Way of Things. From a friend's friend."

Elisabeth squinted, twisted her lips. "That is not a
commonly used phrase, my dear girl. Is this friend another
witch?"

"No, no. He was a normal man. A lovely man. He believed
in the Way and tried to use it to help others. Or so he said. I'm
not quite sure." She pulled away from Elisabeth and fidgeted
with her fingers. "He was murdered. With magic."

"My stars."

"At least that's what Hasis said."

Elisabeth sat up. Her eyes ignited with recognition. "Hasis?" she asked. "Atrahasis?"

"Yes. I think that's what he said. Do you know him?"

Elisabeth kissed the palm of her hand and raised it to the ceiling. "Thank you," she whispered. "The Way is impressive, is it not?" She laughed. "Hasis is a dear friend. One of the only Immortals in this city, in this country! You are blessed to have made his acquaintance."

Every moment spent with that woman cleansed Rita's spirit. For years she felt heavy with the burden of her Sight, with questions about her purpose, but Elisabeth was lifting those worries. She felt renewed. She had many doubts about Hasis. Was he Immortal? Did his ritual summon something sinister? Could he be trusted? Elisabeth had brushed those worries away. He was telling the truth. About everything. That meant he was right about Vincent's death. Magic was indeed the culprit. "You must help me."

"Of course, child. What is wrong?"

"My friend was killed with magic. We must discover who did it so justice can be seen, and peace can be brought to those who need it."

Elisabeth chewed on her bottom lip and rubbed her knees. Her attention was momentarily elsewhere. "We can use the spirit board," she said, standing. She clasped her hands and examined the room. "Now, where is it?"

Rita, too, glanced around the apartment. Until several minutes prior, she had no recollection of being there before. But certain things, like the herringbone floor and the faded pink wallpaper, began to float to the surface of her memory. She closed her eyes and inhaled the stale air, hoping to summon more images from the past. She grazed the fabric underneath her with her fingers, running her hand across the flat cushion until it reached a new texture, a familiar one. She took it in her fist and allowed herself to luxuriate in the exhilarating feeling of recalling the orange crocheted blanket her mother's ghost draped on her when she was upset. She could remember holding it for comfort as Aunt Carrie became angry. And she recalled how weighty it felt on her tiny shoulders as she cried, how it felt like something when her mother's hands felt like nothing.

She resurfaced from the memory with a gasp.

"It was traumatic for you," said Elisabeth. "Becoming aware of your Sight and losing your mother." She removed a long, thin box from the shelf. "It is no wonder you forgot about me." She went to a drawer and pulled out a smaller square box. "But you are still young and able to learn."

"I will be a witch, like you?"

"Yes. It is the Way of Things. You will be a great witch. But first we must get this murder mystery cleared up." She nodded at a cluttered table in the corner. "Clean that so we can work."

Rita rushed to the table and began to pile books and papers in stacks.

"No," Elisabeth said. Her speech was suddenly clipped and powerful. "Use magic. I know you can."

She stopped suddenly, as if she'd been told she'd been gardening in poison ivy. "All right." Her mind was already getting tired from dredging up the past. She didn't know if she could recall the certain kind of telekinesis Vincent had taught in meetings. She tried to begin reciting a charm but felt too lethargic to actually form a sound.

"Magic can be made without words, my dear. The intention behind the spell is all that matters. You are already powerful, so intent will suffice."

This felt like a test. Rita didn't like that. She had had

enough pressure put on her years ago in ballet class. Her instructor had a fondness for singling Rita out, knowing her long feet and knobby limbs refused to cooperate. She remembered many tearful walks home afterward. But now she was famous for embracing her oddness, for dancing with her heart and not according to stiff Renaissance traditions. She had a desire to return to that class and Charleston all over that woman's toes. It was Elisabeth's turn to see how wonderfully uncommon Margarite Duff could be.

She inhaled and fixed her eyes on the tabletop. It was a mess with junk similar to the sewing table she'd cleared earlier at home. She thought of how many separate objects she'd have to focus on, pick up, and relocate. It would take all evening. While that would complete the task set before her, it wouldn't be impressive. So she zeroed in on the parts of the tabletop that weren't covered and let the trinkets around it blend together into one blurry mass. In her mind's eye, she imagined that the junk sat on an invisible tablecloth. She reached out and pantomimed grabbing it by two corners and folding it, like one would do with a blanket after finishing a picnic. As she did this, the objects fell to the center of the table. She raised her hands, lifting the collection, and motioned it toward Elisabeth. With a nod, the rubbish fell into a pile at the old witch's feet.

Elisabeth stared at the floor with wild eyes. She raised her face to look at her new pupil. "Splendid," she said. Her voice was filled with awe and a touch of fear. "Absolutely splendid."

From the long box came the spirit board. It didn't look like the one she'd seen at shops and parties. This one appeared older and included additional markings beyond the usual English alphabet, *yes, no, hello,* and *good-bye.* Elisabeth pulled the planchette, the tear-shaped device with a small window in the middle used to maneuver around the board, out of the smaller box. It was made of polished stone and engraved with what looked like hieroglyphics. She placed it over an illustration of the sun, the hole in the middle allowing its somber face to peer through. "We will both rest our hands on this and let the spirits give us guidance."

Rita surveyed the room. "There aren't any ghosts here."

Elisabeth let out an irritated growl. "Remember what I told you. Not all spirits can be seen, even by us. For instance, your aunt."

Rita had to remind herself that just because she'd been living with her Paramount her whole life didn't mean she knew everything there was to know about it. She couldn't get annoyed when someone with more experience corrected her. She had many things to learn, and she had to be open to accepting guidance. She put her hands on the planchette and nodded at Elisabeth.

Her teacher grinned and joined her. "Now concentrate," Elisabeth said. "Clear your mind and focus solely on the window at your fingertips." She watched Rita to ensure she followed directions. "Spirits!" Her voice climbed to a new register, as if she were onstage at Shakespeare's Globe. "We are witches, keepers of sacred knowledge and devoted followers of the Way." Then she recited the same sentence in a different language, one Rita couldn't place. After living in a neighborhood like the one she resided in, she thought she had an ear for basically everything. Apparently not. Elisabeth must have noticed her confusion. "The older ones only answer in their tongue, my dear. You will learn." She winked. "Ask your question."

She blushed. Why was she feeling shy all of a sudden? Usually when she practiced any kind of magic, she was confident. Being in the presence of a true witch was grating on her poise. Her teeth practically chattered as she spoke. "My friend, Vincent Croft, was m-murdered with magic. He was also a follower of the Way. I want to know who killed him." As Elisabeth repeated the question in the ancient language, Rita's eyes remained fixed on the window. She waited for it to move, to spell out a name.

The planchette felt as if it had been charged with electricity. It didn't sting or shock, but had a certain life about it. It trembled, causing Rita to almost throw her hands in the air. Elisabeth put pressure on her fingers to let her know it was safe, that she needed to be strong. The stone triangle shifted. It glided away from the sun, to the right side of the board. Then it dropped down to the alphabet. It stopped on *W*. Then up to *H*. It finally rested on *Y*.

"Why," Rita said. "Why?"

Elisabeth hummed. "Why do you need to know?" She looked into Rita's eyes. "In the old days, the penalty for inflicting harm on others with magic was death. We no longer live like that. What will you do to his assassin?" She almost purred as she spoke. Her voice was seductive, threatening, and mysterious. Just like her question.

"I don't know. Surely there's a council or something to bring this person in front of."

"Our government has disbanded. Institutes of learning closed. The wars of men were not kind to our kind. It is up to us, to your generation, to usher in a new age." She inhaled long and slowly through her thin lips. Her chin rose, and she gritted her teeth. "What will you do?"

Rita tried to come up with an eloquent answer, but frankly she didn't know how she'd react once she discovered the name of the killer. It'd be difficult no matter who it was, as it was destined to be someone from the Circle, someone everybody trusted. It might be easy...no, not easy. Never easy. It'd be *easier* if it was someone she wasn't close with, like a cast member from anther show. She'd be absolutely devastated if it was a friend, like Harold or Clarissa. Over the last few days, she'd gone through every person she knew and examined their possible motives for harming Vince. She realized everyone could find a reason to cause ill. All people have those feelings at some point or another. But rarely do they escalate to a place where action is taken.

"Margarite?" asked Elisabeth. "What will you do?"

"Something," she said. Her voice was dark and deep. "Believe me."

The stone rattled again.

Elisabeth laughed with excitement. "This is it."

The planchette jerked around the board, sliding their hands with such ferocity Rita feared her wrist would break. Still, she kept her eyes fixed on the round window on the stone. As the letters in the name of Vincent's killer appeared in that space, she panicked. The blood in her face retreated to her heart, sinking it to her belly button. The air in her lungs seeped out like a pin had been stuck in her side. She blinked her eyelids rapidly, making the room look like a movie house when the projector fires up. But instead of seeing Mayer or Fox's name in front of her, she saw hers: *D U F F*

❖

She couldn't do anything until the moon was full. "This phase," Elisabeth said, "is when the nature's energy is greatest. A very powerful time. You will need it to cast out what haunts you." That meant enduring through four days of knowing she was somehow responsible for Vincent's death, Sal's depression, and the upheaval of everyone's lives at the theater. And four days of permanent chills down her spine and raised hairs knowing something lurked nearby, maybe even within her. Those were the longest days of her life.

She recalled fainting once or twice. Sometimes her dreams were lucid. Her imagination veered toward the overactive. She never bothered worrying about them because she thought everyone experienced them sometime during life. But maybe those were the opportunities evil forces took advantage of. How else could she unknowingly muster the kind of magic that could kill a man, especially in the way she'd apparently killed Vincent?

Possession.

Whenever the thought arrived, she had to banish the idea from her mind. It scared her. The more she pondered it, the more she felt evil secreting from her pores, eyes, and ears. How did the entity get inside her?

When you invited me in.

She groaned, shook the thought away. But it wouldn't budge. She wasn't the one who beckoned the entity from the other side. Vincent did. She just helped.

You are guiltier than him. You taught him how to lift the veil.

"No!" she shouted. A passerby glanced at her with concern. She smiled and looked at the ground. It was finally the day of the full moon. She just had to make it through rehearsal, which started at ten. She was running late. "Just a few more hours," she murmured to herself. "I'll see Hasis at sundown. He'll cleanse me." She ran down Forty-Third Street toward the stage door. The ground was slick from a drizzle of rain. The sky was cloudy. "I hope we can see the moon later."

Even if he succeeds, do you deserve to live after what you have done?

Rita slapped her forehead. "Stop."

She threw open the heavy metal door, signed in with Eric,

and ascended the stairs to the attic studio. The room was lined with small, round windows. A gaggle of chorus girls chatted in the corner. One of them laughed. Rita hadn't laughed in days and felt crazy with envy.

"Good Christ," Clarissa said. Her face was contorted with disgust. "What happened to you?"

Rita glared at her, threw down her purse and went to work unbuttoning her giant coat. "Nice to see you, too."

Clarissa took her by the arm and led her to the corner. "You look a wreck. Are you well, darlin'?"

She contemplated telling her everything, but she didn't. "I haven't been sleeping." She took off her coat, revealing what looked like a mourning dress.

Again, Clarissa scowled. She sniffed. Her eyes watered. "Have you bathed?"

"Yes, I have. But I'm wearing garlic."

"Oh, dear. Is this Vincent stuff finally sinking in?" Clarissa looked to the girls to make sure they weren't listening. "Not all these people know about the Circle. Keep the preventative hocus pocus to a minimum."

Rita clenched her jaw. "Magic killed him. What I did killed him."

"You didn't do anything. He'd eventually have found a way to reach the other side with or without you. Those spirits he tangled with killed him. He was too ambitious."

The world was full of half-truths. All the ideas of magic and life and death were muddied by misinformation. Clarissa's opinions were no different. The entity killed Vince. But it carried out the deed through Rita. Her powers crushed him and left him lifeless in that dressing room downstairs. She murdered him. It was her fault.

Clarissa was hugging her. "My goodness, why are you crying?"

Crying? She didn't recall getting upset. Her voice quivered. "I think I'm losing my mind."

Salvatore interrupted by slamming a bench in front of the piano. He flung open the lid to the keyboard with too much force. "Are we ready?" he asked. His face was gaunt. He'd always been thin, but now he looked downright ill.

Clarissa gave Rita's arm a supportive squeeze as she walked to the piano for vocal exercises. Rita stayed in the back of the room, self-conscious about her appearance and smell.

Her mind was crumbling. Whenever she was left alone, she thought about how she did it. When she did it. She took a nap before every performance at about four o'clock. Was that when it happened? Did she rise from her bed in a trance and perform the rite? Or maybe she astral projected. She'd read about that once. Oh, the things humans were capable of in their sleep without knowing. These thoughts had kept her from slumber ever since she saw her name spelled out on Elisabeth's board. As they sang scales, her eyes became heavy. She was desperate to rest.

"Are we not stimulating, Miss Duff?"

She snapped to attention.

Sal was leaning over the piano, staring her straight in the eyes. Did he know?

"I'm fine.*" Miss Duff?* Since when did he use formalities with her? "I apologize."

He cleared his throat and sat down. "The new song," he said. "From the first chorus. It debuts tonight, so I hope you've all got it right by now. Or else you should consider another job."

The girls exchanged confused, nervous glances.

He poked the keys with his fingers. Everyone took a collective breath and sang. "Once I loved you..." Their heads bobbed for four beats. "Oh, how that's changed..."

Sal growled. "You sound like a chorus of corpses."

Four more beats. They sang louder. "The streets we walked now seem strange."

He hit the keys with his fists. "Did Vincent's so-called depression transfer over to all of you? Will you too be dead by curtain?" He ran his fingers through his messy hair. "It's unbelievable how you sound. We went through these harmonies twice last week. It's like listening to a massacre of choking crows." He gathered his sheet music and kicked the stool away. "If you won't take this show seriously, I won't either. Sink or swim on your own tonight." He stormed out.

Clarissa turned around to look at everyone. "We weren't that bad, gals. I don't think he was even playing the right song." She made a point to look everyone in the eye. "You all better go home and get some rest. I don't want to look like a fool tonight because you're all too hungover and depressed to do your jobs." Her series of stares ended with Rita. She raised her eyebrows at her and walked out.

❖

The thick, heavy clouds looked like sponges filled with brackish water. They blocked the sunlight, creating a day that seemed to be perpetually at dusk's doorstep. Hasis's northern forest was alien in that light. The confusing mixture of rain and snow did nothing to help Rita's sight as she attempted to navigate through once-clear pathways. On her last visit to the cave, she'd bounded through the woods with the speed and agility of a deer. Now she slowly stomped with an elephant's clumsiness. She half expected trees to crack and fall in her wake.

She wasn't due to meet Elisabeth and Hasis until nightfall, but she couldn't bear waiting any longer. That entity needed to be exterminated as soon as possible. At least being in the presence of Hasis would bring her comfort. He could draw circles of salt and burn sacred smoke to keep the spirit at bay, and prevent her from falling under another evil influence.

A chill shook the breath from her. She couldn't tell if it was an actual chill from the cold or one sent by a nearby entity. She knew if she turned around there wouldn't be a creature standing there because these things weren't of the physical realm, but she whipped her head around to check her back anyway. As predicted, she was alone. The only movement came from branches swaying to a wind song.

"Get yourself together, Rita," she said, leaning against the trunk of an ancient oak. She looked up to the canopy. Spring had tried to show itself in little chartreuse buds, but this storm robbed them of their color. The forest itself appeared to be cringing its way through winter's last stand. Her thoughts momentarily wandered to Shakespearean plays where personal turmoil manifests itself in some kind of natural fury. "How fitting."

Extremely. Her joints locked, and she held her breath to listen. *These tales often end in death.*

"You've already done that."

No. The voice said. *You did.*

She ran. Not like running would help her escape. The spirit had imprinted itself on her...in her...near her. Whatever it had done, they were attached. Running from it meant running with it. She fought desperately for control of her mind, fearing it would overrule free will and she'd fall. "Hasis!" The path had disappeared. She was meandering aimlessly over boulders and around trees. "Hasis, please help!" She spotted a familiar rock formation on a hillside. The cave wasn't far. With one deep inhalation, she mustered all her strength to push through the entity's taunting and make it to Hasis's door.

She stumbled across the slate floor, over a pile of ash and scattered stones. Lightning illuminated the sky. "Hasis," she panted. "Hasis, where are you?" She kicked the soot from her heels and wandered to his giant bird cages. The twisted vines and twigs forming the crude entrapments had been torn apart. Birds were no longer held prisoner there.

A shadow appeared. "He is gone," said a voice. It was Elisabeth. Rita turned toward the entrance of the cave. The old witch held open the drapes to show the vacancy inside. "He left."

"Where to? Will he be back?"

"No." Her voice was hoarse and tired. "Gone back to Europe, I suspect. Prague. He has abandoned me."

"You?" asked Rita. "He abandoned you? He's supposed to help me." She staggered to her. "I have an entity fighting for control of my mind, of my body. He needs to help me."

Just as Rita was about to grab for her arm and sob, Elisabeth jerked away. "Gather your wits. There's no danger here."

"It's in my head. I hear it fighting for control."

Elisabeth ducked into the cave. Rita followed her in. A lamp burned on an empty table. Bowls, vials, and jars were broken all over the floor. "He made sure to destroy everything." She kneeled to sift through the debris.

"Why aren't you listening to me?" She pushed the heels of her hands against her eyes. "I'm afraid if we don't do something soon, I'll be entirely possessed and do more harm."

"Damnit!" she yelled. "You are well." She hurled an empty jar into the wall. "Nothing haunts you."

"That's impossible. The spirit board. The voices…"

"That board is a hoax. I moved it. And those voices are yours and yours alone. You convinced yourself." She stood and brushed off her dress. "I cannot believe he deserted us like this."

The shivers Rita felt from the cold were overrun by shivers of anger. The fog that'd developed in her head over the last four days cleared. "You had my trust and you manipulated me."

"To protect you. I needed to get you away from that theater so you might join this cause." Elisabeth's shoulders heaved violently. She cried an unintelligible word and wept into her hands. "But he left us alone in this wretched city. Friends for years and he leaves." She blinked her eyes to dry her tears and growled. "We were supposed to do great things!" Her voice blasted around the tiny room.

"You're crazy." Rita went to the curtain. "I need to get downtown."

"He will kill you."

She stopped. "What?"

"This is larger than you, my girl."

"Who are you talking about?"

"Things are changing. You are all part of it."

A tiny bomb of anger exploded in Rita's chest. She pounded the air with her fists, and the contents of the room levitated. "Tell me!" She waved her arms again and everything crashed to the ground.

Elisabeth coughed through a cloud of dust. "Yes, you have power." She stretched her gangly arm toward the girl. "Stay with me. I will teach you to harness it."

Rita's stare was icy. She was sure to look at her long enough to ensure the old witch knew their brief relationship was finished. Then she went through the curtain into the storm.

Elisabeth barreled after her. "Salvatore. It is Salvatore. He will kill you if you leave here."

The rain had turned to snow. Small flurries danced by Rita's face, landing on her eyelashes. *Salvatore.* She tried to understand why he'd do such a thing. *Salvatore.* She blinked the flakes away as she faced Elisabeth once more. "He wouldn't do that."

"To bring back his lover he would." She smoothed the precipitation into her hair. "Forced life requires forced death." She smirked. "And because Vincent was a man of power, Salvatore will have to kill more than a baby bird to bring him back."

"Can that really happen? Will that raise the dead?"

Elisabeth shrugged. "We will find out soon enough. Sacrifice is the oldest form of magic. These Dark Rites are not enacted often." She walked forward. "Come moonrise, the inhabitants of the Duchess Theatre will let us know how much power the Way still has."

Rita lost her breath, like she'd been hit in the back with a paddle. She moved to leave.

Elisabeth held her hand up to stop her. "Ever since I met you, I knew we would meet again. You would be my ward. But the thought of raising you in these conditions, it made me sick. The world has changed, and the Way is not respected. *We* are not respected. But you have helped us make it possible to usher in a new dawn."

Rita's shoes were stuck to the floor. The more she struggled, the more Elisabeth focused her energy on keeping her where she was. Rita gave up. "I didn't help you do anything. I don't even know you."

"No horsemen will sweep through the land. There is no Leviathan sleeping under the sea. Mankind will bring itself to its knees. The veils you taught Vincent to lift unleashed beings that have been trapped on the other side for centuries. They will meddle. They will influence. They will help man find the chaos he needs to fall."

Rita sank to her knees on the wet ground. "I tried to tell Vincent the spells Hasis gave him were trouble." She cried. "I felt it."

"A lesson in trusting your instincts," Elisabeth said with a laugh. "If a witch has any power, it is that."

"We didn't bring just any old spirits over, did we?" Rita lifted her face to meet Elisabeth's. "We summoned demons."

Elisabeth nodded.

"And they killed him."

"No." Elisabeth was quiet. She breathed deeply to secure her hold on Rita. Then she spoke plainly and quickly, obviously struggling to hide all her emotion. "That was indeed magic. My magic. A crushing spell. Usually forbidden. But harsh times call for harsh measures."

"But he was no threat to you." Rita narrowed her eyes. "He was a follower of the Way."

"I am not proud of it, my dear." She cleared her throat, rolled her shoulders into a confident stance. "Another Sacrifice for our cause. You are young, but one day you will know what a powerful force love is. And Salvatore's love for Vincent is very strong. It will start a war here while the demons infiltrate other places."

With all her might, Rita funneled her strength into standing up. Elisabeth's hand was still before her, emanating an invisible, magical energy. Without even making contact with her body, she felt it press her with the force of a raging current. Still, she attempted to find the power to rise. She searched for power in her body. Where did it lie? She had stomped her foot and broken glass at Sal's apartment. She had slammed her arms and threw Hasis's cave into disarray.

Her power was in her arms and legs and was tied to emotion. Anger. Frustration. Finding those sentiments was not difficult. She'd been manipulated. Her friend had died. Love would be used as a force of destruction. Her heart became warm. She could feel the veins in her wrists and ankles become hot, pulsing with charged blood that carried true magic to her fingers and toes. She pressed them into the rock.

The ground grumbled. A tremor startled Elisabeth. She flailed, releasing Rita from her entrapment on the floor.

"You bitch." Rita pushed her hand toward Elisabeth's face and forced the same strength on her. The hag flew backward, but just for a second. She caught her footing, extended her arm, and returned the gesture. The two witches stood palm to palm in combat mode.

With violent, guttural screams, they summoned all the magic within themselves to bring one another down.

"You are a fool, girl!" said Elisabeth. "I am older." She stepped forward. "I am more powerful." She forced Rita to step backward. "I have studied under Immortals!"

Rita panted, mustered more strength, and regained her ground. "Immortals that abandoned you!"

Elizabeth screeched and threw her hand closer in Rita's direction. A massive power exploded from her, causing Rita to slide over the slate floor as if it were a frozen pond.

She glanced behind her and saw she was drawing closer to the cliff. "No!" She pounded the ground with her foot a yard from the edge. Her heel plowed through rock until she was knee-deep in a new trench. With the continuous pressure from Elisabeth's magic and her leg half underground, she fell backward and was forced to lower her hands to break the fall.

Elisabeth paused to observe the helpless girl on the ground in front of her. She grinned. Her eyes were bloodshot, and her usually neat hair had been blown from its bun into a tumbleweed of gray and white. "I hate to lose a witch with so much potential," she said. "But you are trouble." She inhaled and brought her hand close to Rita's forehead. "Good-bye."

Rita could see the power radiate from Elisabeth's palm, twisting the very air between them. She'd read about near-death experiences before, how time slows down and life flashes before one's eyes. She prepared herself to see her home on the other side of the ocean, the boat ride, her aunt crying, her first dance class, her debut on Broadway, her first time with a man...and a woman. Unfortunately, no such visions came to her. That moment before death was just as quick and detailed as real life. But something within her felt new, felt *different*. A sensation of peace, of acknowledging defeat and Death's approach, surged through her. Just as Elisabeth's magic touched her forehead, she closed her eyes and allowed a tiny smile to spread across her face.

A scream pierced her ears. It was a nasty, brutal cry that forced her eyes back open.

Elisabeth's hand came flying at her face and landed in her lap.

It was Rita's turn to scream. Blood sprayed all over her body. Through the spurts, she could see Elisabeth's twisted face howling in pain. Her arm had been lopped off at the elbow. She tried to cover the wound with her other hand, but torrents of blood shot it away every time it came near.

She continued screaming until two hands appeared on her face, jerked it to the right, and snapped her neck. Elisabeth fell to the ground.

Rita yanked her foot out of the hole, slid back, and huddled into a ball.

"Watch out! Don't get too close to the edge."

Rita halted and looked up. It took a few seconds for her eyes to adjust to the curtain of snow. She wiped her face with her sleeve, careful to remove all the blood from around her eyes. "Vincent?"

The ghost nodded. Snowflakes passed through him and landed on her.

She crawled to her knees. "I thought you'd have passed over by now," she said.

"I needed to stick around to find out what's going on." He kneeled. "Thank you for being a good friend. I'm sorry I got you dragged into all this."

Rita shook her head and sniffed back tears. "We must fix things."

"You'll have to do that alone."

"No. I don't know enough about the Way yet."

"Just talk to Sal for me." He glanced around. "I have to go. I've put off crossing over long enough, and they'll be coming for me soon."

Rita also looked at the surrounding area. "Who? The demons?"

He smiled. "No. You'll find out when you have proper training from a good, kind instructor."

"I don't know if that exists. It all seems very corrupt."

"It will be hard to find anything that isn't." He put his hand on her face. It was even cooler than the winter air around her. "Keep faith. You're destined to be a champion of the Way. You'll do great things." He stood and walked toward the woods. "Oh, and Rita?"

"Yes?"

"I've tried reaching out to Sal, but he's too clouded." He seemed to be crying, if a ghost could do such a thing. "So just tell him I know. I know he loves me. I'll be watching him. Always."

❖

Rita muttered to herself the entire time the cab traveled downtown. "Don't be too late. Don't be too late…" Once at Forty-Third Street, she threw money at the cabbie and hurled herself out of the car. "Don't be too late…" There weren't any sirens or crowds nearby to distinguish some kind of trouble at the Duchess. Yet.

She threw open the heavy stage door. Eric was posting something on the call board. "Eric!" she said.

He turned. "Hello, Ms. Duff…" He probably would have said more, had some news about a rehearsal or a cue, but instead he yelped.

She'd forgotten how terrifying she must have looked. "I'm sorry. I know." She patted him on the shoulder. "Is Sal here yet?"

He struggled for words. "A…a…he…a…"

"Holy hell, man. Tell me!"

He scurried to the call sheet and searched for his name. "Yes. Got here thirteen minutes ago."

"We need to find him. He's going to—" She thought for a moment. She didn't want to start a panic and turn this into a witch hunt. That would be exactly what Hasis wanted. She would find Sal and talk to him. They could pretend the whole thing never happened or was never going to happen. She smiled and continued. "He's going to screw up my entrance, I know it. I need to have a chat with him before show time." She raced by him to the stairwell.

"All right, Ms. Duff." Eric squinted, trying to decipher what mess she was covered in. "Have a good show."

"Sal!" Rita hollered over and over again as she clamored up the stairs to the stage level. She threw herself against the steel door and stumbled into the wings. "Sal!"

"Watch it, cookie." Clarissa held her arms up. "What's the hurry?"

There were so many people around. Of course. The curtain went up in ninety minutes. Everyone was getting dressed and warming up and stretching against walls. "I...I..." Rita was having trouble catching her breathe and organizing her thoughts. Could she tell Clarissa? Surely. She knew all about the Way and what really caused Vince's death. And she adored Sal. She'd want to help. Rita grabbed her wrist. "We need to find Sal."

Clarissa finally got a decent look at Rita. She sneered. "What the hell happened to you?"

Rita squeezed harder, gritted her teeth. "It doesn't matter. We're all in danger."

She shivered. "Rita, darling, your eyes just lit up. Bright green."

Rita's fingers and toes began to tingle with heat. "No," she said, pulling away. She had to keep her emotions in check. So much magic had been built up and utilized in the last hour, and more simmered, ready to be poured out. *Breathe. Just breathe.* The sensation faded.

"I don't know where he is. I tried to pull him aside to run a verse, but he bolted. Ran right up the stairs."

Rita turned around and pulled open the door she'd just barreled through. She looked back. "Come on."

They ran to a small elevator at the end of the hall. The doors opened right away. Rita slid open the gate and motioned for Clarissa to enter. She loaded herself on, pulled the lever, and waited to hear the gears churn. When they started to rise, she looked to the ceiling, smiled, and let out a giant sob.

Clarissa stared, horrified at the mess her friend was in. "You need to tell me what's going on."

"He's going to kill everyone. Some batty idea to bring back Vince."

"My God."

"It's not Sal. I mean it is, but he's been manipulated or it's mind control or…" *Breathe, Margarite. Calm down.* "We just need to stop him."

"How do you propose we do that?"

The elevator lurched to a halt. The doors opened.

"Good evening, ladies." Salvatore stood on the other side of the gate. His voice was flat and quiet. "Shouldn't you be getting dressed?"

Clarissa grabbed Rita's hand. "We need to speak to you, chickadee."

Rita noticed him adjust his coat. It was bulkier than usual. She tore open the gate and stepped through. They were nose to nose. "Shouldn't you be in the pit warming up?" Her gaze was intensely set on his brown eyes. In them, she saw a flash of emerald. It wasn't clear if his were igniting or merely a reflection of hers. Either way, they were in trouble.

He laughed a laugh that was deeper than any sound she'd ever heard come from him. He opened his jacket and showed them a parcel wrapped in brown paper. "I was just about to deposit this down the elevator shaft. It spans the entirety of the building. I thought it'd be the best place." He didn't blink, not once. His eyes danced from side to side, but somehow always remained focused on Rita. "You know, because explosions tend to blow upward." Again, he laughed that awful laugh.

"You don't have to do this."

"I do, though." His voice quivered. "I need him back."

"It won't work."

Sal pressed his forehead to hers. He raised his voice and spoke with quick, sharp enunciation. "Of course it is possible." Spit flew from his mouth and onto her face.

She tried to keep her tone calm and neutral. "You don't know that."

Sal stepped backward and grabbed the box from his

coat. He raised it into the air. "I do. An Immortal taught me. Hear that? An Immortal. He's older and more powerful than anything we've ever known or seen."

"No, Sal. He's using you."

"You're just jealous. You're jealous that a regular man, not a witch, can perform such a Rite. I'll bring back the Complete Man and become a wizard myself. Everyone will be forced to accept us."

Clarissa stepped out of the elevator. "Sal, we do accept you."

He was hysterical again. "Not you! *Them!* Get out of my way." He ripped the package open, black powder trickling out of the tear.

Without even thinking, Rita threw her hand and thoughts forward, tearing the box from his grasp, down the hall, and out the door. It landed outside in the snow on the roof terrace. The gunpowder would be ruined.

Sal cried and made a run for it. Rita followed. "Stop. Sal. Wait!"

He turned, mumbled something, and pointed back at them.

Rita flew backward into Clarissa. They exchanged baffled glances and clambered to their feet.

When they reached the door, they found Sal standing over the box, laughing again. The terrace was still tented, the curtains still closed. The spilled powder was perfectly dry. His cackles transformed into a charm in an old language. He waved his fingers. The gunpowder rose off the floor, shaped itself into a sphere, and floated between them.

"Please," Clarissa said, "don't do this."

Tears streamed down his face. "I'm sorry. Really I am." He whispered an inaudible charm, and tiny flames formed on the ends of his fingers. He flicked his wrists and shot the fire toward the sphere.

Rita watched him launch the blaze like tiny comets headed for a dark planet. A fire of her own ignited in her heart. In a fraction of a second, it spread to her limbs. She jumped, stretching her hands and legs as far away from her as she could, creating a blast with enough force to blow the tent above them fifty feet into the sky. A deluge of rain and snow and sleet soaked everything that was once dry.

A moment later, the metal poles that held up the canvas tent came crashing down around them. The first one fell where the sphere had been, the second and third landed on the glass-encased garden theater nearby. The rest plummeted to the street. Screams from pedestrians echoed from below.

Rita was crouched in the center of the terrace. When she was able to refocus her eyes, she saw Sal huddled in a ball, shaking and weeping against the wall. She scurried to his aid. "Sal, are you okay?" She reached for him.

"Please!" He convulsed. "Leave me alone."

She ignored him, grabbed his shoulders and forced him to look at her. "Hasis is a monster. There was a reason he lived all alone in the woods. He's dangerous. He's using you to start trouble."

Salvatore couldn't even form words. He'd deteriorated into a mess of shame and grief and helplessness. He looked to the sky and screamed or cried or something else too distressing for Rita to watch. She heard him cough and gag on rainwater. "I'm sorry." Another wail. "It hurts so much." He buckled into the wall and cried some more.

"What does? Are you injured?"

Somehow he let out a chuckle, a light one like she was used to hearing. "No, I'm not. I'm fine." He was quiet for a second. "I'm alone. It's too painful to bear."

"You've got us." She looked back to find Clarissa limping to their side. "You've got us."

He raised his head and looked at her solemnly. "You know that isn't the same." He searched the wall for the ledge, pulled himself up on it and looked out over the city. Through the rain it was just a blur of lights. He sighed.

Clarissa coughed again. "You won't always be lonely," she said. "You'll meet someone new one day. When you're ready."

He shook his head. "You have no idea what it's like for gentlemen like me. We're hard to find because we aren't allowed to exist. And if you are lucky enough to find someone, who's to say he's a match. And even if he is, what are we reduced to, huh? Meeting in secrecy? Masquerading as something we aren't to get by? Watching him hold the hand of a woman he doesn't even know to throw off suspicion? And then be expected to do the same?" He sat on the ledge and held his head in his hands. "No. That's not for me."

Rita fought through tears to say something, even though she didn't know what to say. So she said the only comforting thing she could think of. "I saw him, Sal." He perked up. "He's watching. He knows you love him. He told me to tell you that."

He grinned so large, it was difficult to decipher if he was laughing or crying. "That's good. That's good." He looked back at the city lights, then back to them. "Then he knows why I need to do this." He looked to the sky and whispered, "I'll see you soon, babe."

Salvatore leaned his head back and tumbled to the street below.

CIRCLE

Spring 1923

"I took what I needed," said Harold. "I don't care about the rest." He threw his cigarette onto the driveway and kicked it around in the gravel.

"It's a shame to lose all that history," Rita said.

"This house was built by greed. Nobody needs to live this way."

Clarissa fanned herself. "I cannot believe you people. You're forgetting the most problematic detail." She widened her eyes for dramatic effect. "It's a godforsaken Hellmouth."

Rita crossed her arms and gazed out the side of her eye. "I apologize for making you go through this."

"Don't even," he said. He laid his hands on her arms. "It wasn't your fault."

"It was, partly."

"We are all to blame. Shouldn't have mucked around in things we didn't know about."

Clarissa agreed with a long hum. "We all wanted power."

Harold Roth's estate was quieter than ever. The help had been let go, the birds sold, and the parties canceled. Spring had arrived and, without the careful attention of several gardeners, the forest had already begun to creep closer and closer, as if it also realized that what resided on that land needed to be hidden. Even with the most beautiful of sunsets behind it, the house emitted darkness.

"When was the last time you went down there?" asked Rita.

Harold chewed on his fingernails, a nervous habit he'd recently developed. "Last week."

Clarissa gasped. "Mr. Roth." She slapped his shoulder.

"I know. I just wanted to make sure it was true. I worked hard for this house. I don't like it, but I worked hard for it." He put his arm around Clarissa. "Something more comfortable will be better for us."

She nuzzled him and practically purred.

When he went into the basement that last time, Harold was amazed at its state. As he opened the door, he was hit with the stench of what seemed like one hundred rotting corpses. After several minutes of gagging, he covered his nose and mouth with a handkerchief and descended the stairs. Black veins of decay spread across the floor. He followed them to their source under the leaky window where the water was to the north and the forest to the south, the place Rita and Vincent performed the ritual that, unbeknownst to them, opened a portal to a mysterious and ancient world. The air was cold and thick. The floor had sunken, filled with black, opaque water. Harold became achy and faint. His disposition turned sour. Before he knew it, he was standing ankle-deep in the small pool. He didn't know how he snapped out of that strange trance, but he was glad he did. He'd burned the clothes he wore that day and hadn't been back in the house since.

A hand landed on his shoulder, yanking him out of the

memory. "Sorry I'm late." Harold gasped. Salvatore stood behind him.

"Oh, it's you," Roth said as he gave him a great bear hug. "You can't creep up on me like that. Especially not here."

"Well, there won't be a here for much longer," said Sal. "Shall we?"

"I'm glad you made it." Rita wrapped her arms around his neck and hung there like a human amulet.

Clarissa kissed his cheek. "You look good." She winked.

He reached down and squeezed both of their hands. "Thank you. Thank you both."

His soul had been damaged, and he didn't have a clue how to begin mending it, if such a thing was even possible. He thought about how many people had experienced similar desperation, had been as broken as he'd felt. On that cold night a week prior, he was positive most of those fractured individuals would have decided to fall away from troubles. So that was what he did.

After Rita and Clarissa saved him, he thought about all the men who walked the earth with heavy hearts with battered spirits. Somehow they carried on. They never made split decisions in moments of sadness like he'd done. They acknowledged that life can be long and arduous and complicated. Human happinesses are not the same; some are elated by money, some by fame, and others by love and family. But every person eventually experiences the same kind of pains. Failure. Humiliation. Loss. Loss especially. Death is inescapable. Salvatore didn't find pleasure in knowing that, but he did find a strange comfort in the thought. All men must persevere through it at one point.

When she saw him fall backward, Rita didn't remember consciously making a move to rescue him. It was instinctual, maybe a primal witch impulse to protect the lives of men. Without realizing it, she reached forward and emanated the strength to catch him midair. She looked to Clarissa. "Help me!"

Clarissa raced to her side and made the same motions. She acted on the same gut feeling. All she could do was focus her energy and thoughts on saving him, on raising him back over the ledge and into their arms.

"I'm going to stop all this bullshit," Clarissa said. "No more chants or spells or supernatural voodoo to help me along. Everything I do will be done by me and me alone. I just wanna sing and dance and screw." She looked at Harold.

Harold nodded. "I think that's an excellent idea."

Rita tapped her foot, struggling to say what she needed to. She puffed her cheeks and blew out air. "I can't do that."

"What do you mean? Magic has done so much harm to us already."

"I've been chosen. I have a responsibility. I want to learn from the right people and restrict my powers only to what I need to do as an assistant, not master, of the Way."

Sal stepped forward and looked at her like they were the only two people there. "How will you do that?"

"Travel. All over creation. Learn from every witch I can. Sift through the good and the bad teachings and get a sense about who I am. I don't think I know quite yet."

"So you're going to leave us?" he asked. "You're going to leave *me*?"

She caressed his cheek. "You're going to be fine, chickadee," she said, looking at Clarissa.

He laughed even though tears were welling in his eyes.

"Madelyn is catching a train home to Kansas this evening," said Rita. "I'm going to tag along. I've never traveled like that before. Then I'll find my way from there. But don't worry. I'll be back."

The sunset caused the sky to grow brighter before night crept in. Harold cleared his throat. "That's our cue," he said. "We should leave before nightfall."

Everyone agreed. They joined hands.

"Now," Rita said. "We are going to make our last spell together a good one. We won't use any of those silly chants. Just our minds. It's possible, right, Clar?" Clarissa smiled and nodded enthusiastically. "Just focus on the house. Imagine the basement. Feel the darkness there. Let it affect you. Let it make you angry or sad or whatever you need to feel. Take that emotion and let it grow."

Rita coached them through their discovery of true magic and, in time, the mansion crumbled. It started with a broken window, then a column near the front door. Soon pieces of it began to blow away with the wind like it was made of nothing but mere sand. Then a spark went off. A great fire rose from the house's center and blazed with colors that shamed the brilliant sky behind it.

❖

He had made pit stops in several cities across Europe, drawing deals and parting veils. His train pulled into its final destination, a city that was once the center of knowledge for all the world's mysteries. He hadn't been there in centuries, since the Institute fell into disgrace. Still, he recognized the smell of the air, the feeling of the stones beneath his feet. He had an instinctual knowledge of where to go, even though some streets had changed, some for better and some for worse. Prague was an ancient place, as old as some of man's gods.

It was steeped in magical energy that he was eager to once again harness. The fatigue he'd felt in America had lifted. His mind was strong. The dawn of a revitalized age for the Way was rising. A new family of powerful Immortals would be organized, and he would be a brother to them all.

About the Author

Jeremy grew up on the Jersey Shore, where his primary life goal was to become a mermaid. When that proved impossible, he decided the next best thing would be to move to New York City and study theater at Marymount Manhattan College. He lived an actor's life for several years before he began writing for the page and for the stage. *Dark Rites* is his third novel.

Learn more at www.jeremyjordanking.com.

Soliloquy Titles From Bold Strokes Books

Dark Rites by Jeremy Jordan King. When friends start experimenting with dark magic to gain power, Margarite must embrace her natural gifts to save them. (978-1-62639-245-8)

Driving Lessons by Annameekee Hesik. Dive into Abbey Brooks's sophomore year as she attempts to figure out the amazing, but sometimes complicated, life of a you-know-who girl at Gila High School. (978-1-62639-228-1)

Asher's Shot by Elizabeth Wheeler. Asher Price's candid photographs capture the truth, but when his success requires exposing an enemy, Asher discovers his only shot at happiness involves revealing secrets of his own. (978-1-62639-229-8)

The Melody of Light by M.L. Rice. After surviving abuse and loss, will Riley Gordon be able to navigate her first year of college and accept true love and family? (78-1-62639-219-9)

Maxine Wore Black by Nora Olsen. Jayla will do anything for Maxine, the girl of her dreams, but after becoming ensnared in Maxine's dark secrets, she'll have to choose between love and her own life. (978-1-62639-208-3)

Bottled Up Secret by Brian McNamara. When Brendan Madden befriends his gorgeous, athletic classmate, Mark, it doesn't take long for Brendan to fall head over heels for him—but will Mark reciprocate the feelings? (978-1-62639-209-0)

Searching for Grace by Juliann Rich. First it's a rumor. Then it's a fact. And then it's on. (978-1-62639-196-3)

Dark Tide by Greg Herren. A summer working as a lifeguard at a hotel on the Gulf Coast seems like a dream job...until Ricky Hackworth realizes the town is shielding some very dark—and deadly—secrets. (978-1-62639-197-0)

Everything Changes by Samantha Hale. Raven Walker's world is turned upside down the moment Morgan O'Shea walks into her life. (978-1-62639-303-5)

Fifty Yards and Holding by David Matthew-Barnes. The discovery of a secret relationship between Riley Brewer, the star of the high school baseball team, and Victor Alvarez, the leader of a violent street gang, escalates into a preventable tragedy. (978-1-62639-081-2)

Tristant and Elijah by Jennifer Lavoie. After Elijah finds a scandalous letter belonging to Tristant's great-uncle, the boys set out to discover the secret Uncle Glenn kept hidden his entire life and end up discovering who they are in the process. (978-1-62639-075-1)

Caught in the Crossfire by Juliann Rich. Two boys at Bible camp; one forbidden love. (978-1-62639-070-6)

Frenemy of the People by Nora Olsen. Clarissa and Lexie have despised each other for as long as they can remember, but when they both find themselves helping an unlikely contender for homecoming queen, they are catapulted into an unexpected romance. (978-1-62639-063-8)

The Balance by Neal Wooten. Love and survival come together in the distant future as Piri and Niko face off against the worst factions of mankind's evolution. (978-1-62639-055-3)

The Unwanted by Jeffrey Ricker. Jamie Thomas is plunged into danger when he discovers his mother is an Amazon who needs his help to save the tribe from a vengeful god. (978-1-62639-048-5)

Because of Her by KE Payne. When Tabby Morton is forced to move to London, she's convinced her life will never be the same again. But the beautiful and intriguing Eden Palmer is about to show her that this time, change is most definitely for the better. (978-1-62639-049-2)

The Seventh Pleiade by Andrew J. Peters. When Atlantis is besieged by violent storms, tremors, and a barbarian army, it will be up to a young gay prince to find a way for the kingdom's survival. (978-1-60282-960-2)

Asher's Fault by Elizabeth Wheeler. Fourteen-year-old Asher Price sees the world in black and white, much like the photos he takes, but when his little brother drowns at the same moment Asher experiences his first same-sex kiss, he can no longer hide behind the lens of his camera and eventually discovers he isn't the only one with a secret. (978-1-60282-982-4)

Meeting Chance by Jennifer Lavoie. When man's best friend turns on Aaron Cassidy, the teen keeps his distance until fate puts Chance in his hands. (978-1-60282-952-7)

Lake Thirteen by Greg Herren. A visit to an old cemetery seems like fun to a group of five teenagers, who soon learn that sometimes it's best to leave old ghosts alone. (978-1-60282-894-0)

The Road to Her by KE Payne. Sparks fly when actress Holly Croft, star of UK soap *Portobello Road*, meets her new on-screen love interest, the enigmatic and sexy Elise Manford. (978-1-60282-887-2)

Swans and Clons by Nora Olsen. In a future world where there are no males, sixteen-year-old Rubric and her girlfriend Salmon Jo must fight to survive when everything they believed in turns out to be a lie. (978-1-60282-874-2)

Kings of Ruin by Sam Cameron. High school student Danny Kelly and loner Kevin Clark must team up to defeat a top-secret alien intelligence that likes to wreak havoc with fiery car, truck, and train accidents. (978-1-60282-864-3)

Wonderland by David-Matthew Barnes. After her mother's sudden death, Destiny Moore is sent to live with her two gay uncles on Avalon Cove, a mysterious island on which she uncovers a secret place called Wonderland, where love and magic prove to be real. (978-1-60282-788-2)